2019

IT'S Wi

iN Room 612!

# INFERNAL GLOW

## CHARLES T. DAUBE

STAY SPOOKY,

Contact the author at charlestdaubebooks@gmail.com.

Cover design by Kealan Patrick Burke at Elderlemon Design

Editing by Jennifer at Jenn Lockwood Editing

ISBN 978-1-7325619-9-1

*To my wife and best friend, Heather, who consistently makes dreams come true.*

*And to you, the reader. Without you, I'd just be talking to myself.*

# INFERNAL GLOW

# PART I

## LUMINESCENCE

## 1

**W**ho is screaming? My weary mind ponders while lying awake in the darkness of a cramped motel. A shout so loud that it must have originated from just behind the paper-thin wall adjacent to my headboard. The faceless shriek lingers in my mind, almost comfortable, like it has always been there.

A damp shirt is plastered to my chest as my lead eyes stare toward the ceiling. My statued expression thinking of nothing, thinking of everything. My outstretched hand is noticeably barren as it rests atop the itchy, wool bedspread.

I lie on an obese mattress where years of visitors have left a part of themselves behind on its rusted-spring torso: dead skin, sweat, mites, and their waste. The material hoards the unconventional souvenirs, becoming heavier, more sluggish than the day it was folded through the doorway.

A grimy breeding ground for hire.

Positioned above, an eggshell-tinted ceiling fan spins on full power, swaying from side to side. Teetering, flirting with the notion of flying off its cheap, brass-coated mounting bracket. With its steady rocking, the fan sings a soft mechanical melody of two metallic pieces rubbing against one another.

*Thump, thump, thump.*

I envision its five spinning arms being released at

lightning fast speeds, jettisoning across the room like ninja stars, and a bleak thought enters my dreary mind: *Would those dust-caked blades have enough force to stick into the wall, or maybe even impale me?*

The fan's sole purpose is to circulate the stale, musty fragrance the room seems to emanate. One of those smells you can be around for days and it will still make your skin crawl. Feeling its existence soak into your clothes, ooze into your pores, seep into your soul. Its yellow stench burrowing into the tiny hairs deep within your nostrils like a diseased flea. The scent revealing the masked truth that although everything appears somewhat clean, it is not. There is an underlying filth which cannot be washed out.

Besides the jarring shout, none of these factors are the reason I cannot get back to sleep. The bachelor life has equipped me with the invaluable skill to be somewhat comfortable in less than favorable living arrangements.

It's not what's inside the room, it's what's *outside.*

A faint, resounding *clink–clink—clink* on the door is causing the peaceful sleep realm to elude me. A sound so subtle that one might not even notice it, but once you *hear* it, it demands your attention. Each *clink* threatens to pierce my eardrum, beating against the walls of my ear canal with the percussion force of a gong. A sporadic, odd sound lacking any apparent rhythm. With each *clink,* I hope it is the last, just to be disappointed seconds later.

*What is that damn noise? All I want is sleep. Is that too much to ask?* My mind recalls that this *is* an outdoor facing room. Could the thunderous sound be the wind blowing the door knocker against its metal plate? *Does my door even have a knocker? I sure as hell didn't bother to notice while shuffling into the room with a bladder ready to burst at the seams.*

*Clink–clink—clink.*

*Thump, thump, thump.*

I refuse to abandon the semi-comfort of my rented bed while the frustration is primed to explode. Red-hot, boiling sensations creep up my neck, traveling farther, spreading their black roots into the loose soil of my brain. Tingling. Infuriating. "SHUT THE HELL UP!"

The sound ceases.

My eyes spring open, staring toward the door in disbelief. *Did that just happen? No, it's not possible to stop something from making a noise by yelling. Unless it's not a* something.

*Someone.*

The sole remaining sound is that of the fan's rhythmic tune of *thump, thump, thump.*

The frigid fingers of fear wrap around the meat of my upper arms. *The door is locked. Nobody can get in here. Unless they have a key. Even if they did, the chain is latched. Nobody is out there. I'm just freaking myself out for no reason. I should be happy; now I can sleep.*

Choking down the unwarranted fear, my hair presses

into the deflated pillow, my thoughts now focused on the soothing knocking of the fan.

The kaleidoscopic, disoriented flash frames of a dream-promising sleep begin to pass before my eyes, but something is wrong. The ceiling fan has skipped a beat. And another. And another. Complete silence fills the room. Sinister silence.

The world on mute.

My dry eyes pry open as sweat bubbles take shape on my neck.

BOOM!

A flood of sound and force crashes against the outer motel door. The door shudders from the vicious assault. The windows rattle within their sashes. The floral-patterned curtains are thrown horizontal with the floor, the drapery suspended in mid-air as if the room has been flipped on its side.

They seem to linger forever in a world without gravity.

The curtains feather back down, fanning against the stagnant air, returning to their natural state.

A bolt of electricity sears down my spine, turning the hot sweat to ice. Paralyzed. Frozen. My hands grip the sheets with such intensity that they may disintegrate into dust.

My stomach remains lodged in my throat. A parched swallow forces it back down. I stare ahead with adamantine eyes, yet not seeing. *No way that was real, right? Please, someone, tell me that didn't just happen.*

I must be dreaming. This must be one of those night terrors or sleep paralysis dreams I've heard about. *Please let this be a dream.* I remain motionless as my heart races, lurching beneath its rib-caged housing, the bony digits restraining an organ that desperately desires to abandon its fleshy home.

No matter how hard I try to wish it away, this is real. *Too* real. I'm forced to accept reality like some cocky beachfront homeowner in the face of an incoming hurricane. Making foolish jokes, spray-painting the names of the storms I'd survived, stocking up on cheap beer. Invincible until the eye sees you. Eating my own defeated words when the winds roll in.

*Thump, thump, thump.*

The fan resumes its rhythm. *Maybe that means it's over... at least for now.*

*I must get out of bed. There will be no chance to defend myself while swaddled in the covers like a newborn.* I muster up a scrap of courage, peeling back the sweat-soaked sheets from my quivering body, but never breaking my stare from the entryway. My body seems magnetized to the wool blanket as it clings to my hairy legs and tangled sheets. A tiny electrical storm brews beneath the covers as miniature lightning bolts crackle and splinter. After wrestling myself free from its grasp, my bare feet silently find the floor. Behaving this way seems ridiculous considering I *just* yelled at the top of my lungs moments ago. Whatever is out there knows I'm in here.

It knows I am alone.

Standing up at the bedside, wearing only an undershirt and a pair of crinkled boxers, I feel vulnerable. Something about not being dressed makes me believe whatever is outside could rip me apart *that* much easier. I could be a well-used candle, my former veiled wax melted to a clear, inedible soup, permitting a full view of my glued wick–all of my inner workings exposed to the world.

The carpeted floor might as well be concrete. Any cushioning it ever possessed disappeared long ago. Pressed down, flattened, and abused throughout its existence by the many inhabitants of this room. Any life it had withered away with each crushing footprint, selflessly sacrificing itself for a stranger's comfort.

*I need a weapon.* While scanning my gloomy surroundings, I now view harmless furniture pieces as potential killing tools. An outdated desk sits along the opposite wall with a tucked-in, tufted chair. On the desk lies a notepad, an advertisement for food that a homeless man would refuse, a large ornate lamp, and a remote. Beside the desk stands a small refrigerator with a discolored microwave seated above. A large tube television sits atop a wooden dresser adorned with tarnished gold drawer pulls.

To my right is a nightstand that supports my wallet and keys. The stand is equipped with a single drawer, which I hope has a loaded .45 caliber handgun hidden within. I reach and pull the drawer handle, the soft moan of the sliding wood echoing throughout the overcast room.

*Creeeak.*

7

Slight movement dashes within the drawer. My eyes squint to focus inside the dark compartment, and the flash moves once again, this time from left to right. My nose inches closer to the abyss.

Then I see it. A massive intrusion of grown cockroaches is revealed, each as black as night with hollow, sapphire eyes. Hundreds of pairs. Each wicked set gleaming toward me. *They are about to lunge out into the room.* I slam the drawer shut, pinching one monstrous pest between the momentum-filled drawer and the stand. A shotgun spray of black gore explodes against my face and torso, reeking of death. Even worse, with my sheer terror and quick movement, I didn't close my mouth—it *tastes* like death, too. I gag and spit on the cheap carpet, eager to vomit.

*I was sleeping beside that?* Usually when you open a cheap nightstand drawer, you find a crisp, unread bible staring back at you, not swollen vermin that pop like infected cysts. *Bad omen.* I attempt to clean my face with my palms. The tacky, peanut-buttery consistency is enough to make last month's dinner resurface. The failed effort only serves to smear it across my cheeks and lips.

I can't imagine what my face looks like now. Maybe I'll open the door and horrify the person on the other side even more than they have terrified me. My own repugnant war paint.

Despite its opportunistic appeal, I elect *not* to throw a handful of disgusting cockroaches at the mysterious villain on the other side of the door—no matter how effective that may be. I'd only wind up vomiting all over the perpetrator like I was in need of an exorcism, which *could* be equally effective.

Instead, I opt for the lamp on top of the desk—big and heavy, but mobile enough to swing around like a psychopath. But first, I need to get there.

Walking barefoot across the carpet, each step is an eternity. At any moment, that door will fly off its rusty, weakened hinges and reveal my killer. The person, monster, or whatever it is that my whole life has been building toward.

*I'm here. I've been waiting on you, Arden. Patiently waiting your entire fucking life. Always watching you, my chin rested against your shoulder. Biding my time for the perfect moment when you are at your weakest. Tonight's the night. Our night. When you will beg me to end it all.* The malicious predator confronting its fragile prey.

The distinction between fear-induced imagination and reality has become indiscernible.

I arrive at the desk after five steps and waste no time grabbing the lamp. Picking it up, it does have good weight. My hands even seem to fit well around its baseball-bat-shaped base. Only, baseball bats don't have giant, party hat lampshades on one end. Turning toward the door, a tug pulls against my weapon—the damn thing is still plugged in. With one swift yank, the cord separates from the wall, transforming the pristine prongs into backwoods teeth. *Sorry, motel, you can charge that to my credit card.*

With my new weaponry and its lifeless cord dragging

behind, I feel ready to approach the door.

Until–

The door chain is *moving*. It travels through the skinny slot, inching toward the open mouth. *This cannot be. Could they be using a magnet to drag the chain from the outside?* The gold links are no longer drooping, but are straightening more with each second. The chain dashes to the left, released from the constraints of its slotted latch. Plunging down like a wrecking ball, its pendulum swing raps against the scarred door trim.

*This is it. They're coming in.* Any sense of protection or safety has vanished. *What could they want from me? I have no money, I doubt they want to rape me, and I haven't bothered anyone.* Unless they don't need money, they don't want sex, and they don't *need* a reason. Their single, twisted pleasure deriving from the moment life departs a victim's eyes.

Using fear as foreplay, lured by the pulsating pheromones, each drenched in delectable fear.

These crazed thoughts are even worse than the dreaded suspense of confrontation.

*The door. I need to get there before this* thing *comes in.* With three panicked steps, I'm there, my back pressed against the wall, wedged between the door and the shaded window.

Listening. Nothing but *thump, thump, thump.*

The door *does* have a peephole—not that I'm eager to glance through just in time to get my face flattened by the blunt force of it shooting out of the frame. A peek out of the curtains reveals plain darkness, almost as if someone painted the outer window black.

I have two options: stay here all night with my embarrassing weapon and attire, *hoping* nothing happens, or open the door.

The biggest part of me is screaming to stay inside the room, wait for the morning, and get the hell out of this roach-infested hole at daylight. *The door is still locked, and I could re-latch the chain. Although, I'm not sure if either will hold if one of those blasts hits again.* All I know is this motel's review rating is going to hell in a handbasket after I'm through with it!

As much as I'd like to stay in here with my new hairy-legged friends, I must see what's out there. I bet it's nothing. Maybe this is all an elaborate flashback trip from when I took mushrooms in high school. *That can happen, right? No, that's LSD. Shit.*

One option remains: opening the door. Reaching toward the handle, an arch of static electricity shoots into my index finger. Searing pain splinters through my hand, releasing a horde of butterflies from the pit of my stomach into my tonsils. *I could have done without that.*

Now free of static buildup, I calm myself, gripping the handle once more. *I can do this. I must do this. I'm an adult. This is what adults do. They investigate noises and deal with problems, not hide from them in their ratty pajamas.*

With one clean motion, I swing the door open, sending it crashing into the wall. My back remains pressed flat, waiting for the intruder to enter, my lamp at the ready. The most suspenseful moment of my life passes, yet nobody appears.

I'm not falling for this trick. I continue to wait.

Another heart-pounding, uneventful minute elapses, the realization setting in that nobody is coming. Poking my head around the doorframe presents an unexpected scene.

There is no burly man. There is no mutant beast—*but something else.*

Despite the lack of a deranged killer, my room no longer opens to a car-filled parking lot. A long hallway lies before me with my room situated at one end. Its distance is immeasurable; the end is not within sight. It stretches forever, tunneling down to a pinpoint of darkness.

A tall, black ceiling reigns over the corridor.

The hallway is well lit despite there being no apparent light fixtures. The walls are a deep crimson red, borderline purple–the color of fresh, tender bruises. Each side of the hallway is lined with numerous, gargantuan-sized wooden doors. I lose count after fourteen.

I could be looking down an infinity mirror, seeing endless boxed versions of myself, each variant shrinking frame by frame. Carbon copies housed within the cube, each a fraction of a second behind the last, all returning my stare. A disturbingly real and vacant glance painted on every face.

The floor is a reflection of the ceiling, so black it is rendered invisible. I extend my right foot across the threshold, tapping the jet-black floor. The surface could be a sheet of ice, lacking any texture, yet warm to the touch on my bare toes. *Seems solid enough.*

This peculiar hallway has my curiosity, to say the least. The magnetism of the corridor draws me out of the room. Standing now with both feet on the invisible floor, the greatest sense of inevitable doom engulfs my soul.

I spin around just in time to have the motel room's door slammed in my face. My slippery palms struggle with the handle, fumbling wildly. Its brushed nickel arm bounces against my grip. My shoulder slams against its seam, my hot breath fogging the paint. It is all for naught; the door is well locked and unwilling to budge.

My frenzied eyes dart toward the location of the room's window, finding nothing but a solid wall. Leaning my forehead against the door, I inhale a long, deep breath. A worthless, feeble attempt to snap myself out of whatever hell I'm in. *Am I losing my mind? None of this makes sense. Why didn't I stay inside the room?*

## 2

Equal parts confusion mixed with crippling anxiety consume my thoughts, riding on the back of every neuron as it speeds along its endless, winding track. I try to bring myself out, to wake myself up, to bring back *some* sense of a normal reality. My eyes pinch tightly as my lungs vacuum and filter the still air. They remain closed as I count down from five.

Four.

Three.

Two.

One.

When they peel back open, nothing has changed.

*How pathetic am I to believe that would work?* My attempts are as futile and cowardly as a keyboard warrior sitting in their snug home, bitching about all of the issues of the world. Giving their take on how life should be lived, but refusing to take action themselves. Justifying that they are doing something by shoving the topic into another's uncaring, blue-tinted face. The comfortable humanitarian. The armchair activist.

The noxious blend of pent-up frustration and overwhelming fear speeds through my veins, coming to a head, itching to be squeezed, ready to pop. With my fist coiled as tightly as a frightened snake, I punch the motel door. I haven't been in many fights in my life, my knuckles are not tempered, but that door could be solid steel. *Big mistake.* Looking down at my trembling hand, a thin stream of blood trickles out of my split open knuckle.

Time slows.

My bright red, liquid filler oozes down my middle finger, forming a large, cartoonish bead. The bloated drop swells to the point where it fractures, descending slowly to the black floor below, reinventing itself from oval to round.

Time stops.

The bloody orb splashes into the blackness. Red mist is haphazardly strewn around the drop location, painting a vibrant, almost artistic, contrast of red on black. Within the blink of an eye, the blood absorbs into the floor.

BOOM!

The lamp drops as I cover my ears, tuck my chin to my chest, pinch my eyes shut, and squat to the floor, bracing for the audial impact. Whatever that noise is, it is much, much louder in the hallway than it was inside the room. Although it was deafening before, the door must have muffled most of the sound.

While hunched down on the floor, I open my eyes, unclench my teeth, and uncover my ears. I can only assume the noise has ceased, because all I hear is the *EEEEEEE!* of my eardrums screaming bloody murder.

*Where is the lamp?* My palms glide along the vacant

floor in a dramatic wiper motion, swishing left, swishing right. I feel nothing but uninhabited coldness as my spinal column twists with enough force to topple the stack. It isn't here; it has vanished. *Did the floor swallow my one means of defense? Of course, it did. Great. Am I next?*

My clouded hearing clears and I decide, *that's enough.* I plop down on my rear, crossing my arms and legs, saying aloud to no one, "That's it. I'm giving up. Whatever—whoever—is coming to kill me can just do it already. Obviously I suck at this, so let's get it over with. Feel free to pop your happy ass out from one of these doors. I won't run. Tell that deafening sound to crank it to eleven, rupture my eardrums, and make me bleed out through my burst ear canals and sunken eye sockets. Screw it, let the floor swallow my ass up, but before you do, let me give you an appetizer." With my cheeks pressed against the slippery floor, I push out a booming, echoing flatulence of defiance. It doesn't come close to rivaling the hallway's power, but it still remains one to be proud of. A chuckle passes through my slanted grin as the rotten smell enters my nostrils.

Just then, a movie plays before my eyes, filled with nonsensical images and hidden meanings. The type of film people claim to love but don't truly understand. The audience misinterpreting every scene, crafting their own meanings, creating their own reality. The muddled director never meaning to be analyzed, but unwilling to argue with being hailed as a genius. Its grip tightens around my vision, leading my susceptible consciousness away like a kite on a taut, sharp string. The spool unwinds ferociously, tempting one to sacrifice some layers of flesh to reel it back.

The clandestine portrayal stars a nameless woman. The opening scene is a candid shot of her running away from me. Her lush, auburn hair swings wildly with each planted step. My eyes are the camera, pursuing the lead, capturing her every breath, desperate to keep her near. I struggle to match her pace as her head turns slightly to the right, exposing the slightest sliver of crescent cheek. A familiar face. A black object falls from her hair. Then another.

*More.*

The objects careen to the floor, pouring from her locks, but I remain focused on the pursuit. The levee inside her ruptures. They fall in waves; so many that they all could be connected. Like a single drop of water, then another, another, until an ocean forms. My feet slip, forcing me on my knees, my hands buried in an endless pile of the black objects. I grab an overflowing handful and attempt to regain my footing as she travels farther. I can no longer move; they have captured my full attention.

*Hairpins.* Millions of them.

I'm surrounded in a churning sea of wavy metal, the raging riptide pulling me under. I fight the hairpins, my arms taking the form of a shovel to push them away. Yet the harder I struggle, the deeper I sink. I breathe the pins in. They fill my mouth, my nostrils, and the capillaries of my lungs. My teeth clench and grind against their shiny backs. The cherry hair is out of sight.

*I always knew these things were dangerous, but I couldn't conceive a more comforting death.*

An invisible hand reaches beneath the tide, and I hear a whisper in the dark. *"Death is her name..."* My mind speaks entirely in metaphors; I can only hope I'm clever enough to decipher them.

A drop of liquid lands square on top of my head, abruptly ending the baffling manifestation before the credits roll.

I look toward the dark expanse of the ceiling, and it is *falling.* An approaching ocean. I only have time to pinch my shoulders against my earlobes as an avalanche of liquid crashes down upon my body, instantly filling the hallway with a foot of standing, cold water.

*I needed a bath.*

I stand and attempt to look upward, but I'm blinded by the sudden downpour of *rain*—the mightiest downpour I've ever witnessed. The drops fall as liquefied hailstones, punching and battering into the water near my knees. Thousands of moisture meteors thrash the tide, pummeling every inch of my frail body. I wouldn't call it a torrential storm. I wouldn't label it violent. There is only one word in the history of our language that could describe its wrath.

*Biblical.*

Sent from above by a deity—the only being in the universe capable of creating such destruction. The strafing assault is clearly devised for a clear mission: to snuff out, to kill. *The impure will pay, the abominations will suffer, and all will atone.*

Within seconds, the water is halfway up my thighs,

inching higher, with no sign of slowing.

*I don't want to drown.* I envision that awful feeling of being without breath. Panicking. Desperately searching for just one more lungful of oxygen, another chance, another second on this planet. Yet, only finding more suffocating water. This will be my future if I stay here any longer. I was willing to be torn apart by some man-beast or ingested by an invisible floor, but not this.

*Maybe the hallway* knows *this and is using this fear to keep me moving.*

With the water now past my waistline and a bomblet exploding against my crown, I begin trudging toward the massive, mysterious doors. I move slowly through the heavy, molasses-like water. *Which door should I choose?* Besides their physical location, each door appears identical to the last.

I wade past the first set of opposing doors without hesitation, deciding it's too obvious to enter those. The second pair doesn't seem right, or even the third. *I must make a choice before it's too late.* I now approach the sixth set of doors as the water splashes around my collarbone. It's hard to believe, but the interior storm is intensifying–time is running out.

*Left or right side? I'm about to die. Does it even matter at this point?* I swim to the right side of the hallway, now situated before my forced destination.

I shouldn't, but I can't help but pause. I knew the doors were gigantic, but now within my reach, it could be its own *world.* The entryway spans upwards of twenty feet high, five feet wide, and stained a dark, coffee brown. My squinted eyes strain to reach the upper trim. The door appears to be fashioned from a singular piece of lumber. There are no breaks in its pattern, all the grain flowing as seamlessly as a flock of migratory birds. I admire the wood's endless growth rings, each as unique as a fingerprint, a mark of wisdom. The inlaid texture tells the story of the tree's lifespan: years of thirst, years of prosperity, its demise.

My hands dive through the churning water, a blind fish searching for a point of entry. My pruned fingertips dance along the wooden flesh, finally locating a pointed, glass doorknob. The knob presses divots into my palm as the fingers enclose its slippery edges. *I hope this isn't locked. I don't know what I'll do.* I give the knob a powerful twist and the enormous door opens inward. Comforting relief blankets every cell of my being.

The water sloshes into my gaping mouth and the splashes blur my vision. *This is it.* I step through the frame and enter the dark expanse of the inner room.

The water does not follow.

I turn back to witness the wall of water hovering in the hallway, rising with every fibrillating beat of my heart. It remains encased in an aquarium. As if that isn't strange enough, I'm no longer *wet.*

*How can this be?* I reach a quivering hand toward the embankment, and it slides into the liquid as a hot knife cuts through slouched, tabletop butter. Its biting wetness soaks my skin, compressing with enough pressure to squeeze a jellyfish stream of blood from my battered knuckle. The swirling waves seem to communicate as they engorge my pores, daring me to return to the hallway, inviting me to surrender while I can.

I retract my arm, revealing dry skin once again. As I stare in dumbfounded amazement at my oscillating hand, the water line silently overtakes the crest of the door. *I guess there's no going back that way.* Fearing that whatever force that holds this expanding sea may give out under the immense weight, I grip the old-growth edge and walk the gigantic door to its frame.

As the mammoth door meets the frame, the audible *click* of the locking mechanism engages. *I'm accustomed to doors locking on me by now, but I'm fine with this one staying closed.*

The suffocating hallway also inhaled the final light. Darkness enfolds me.

FLASH!

The room illuminates with blinding fluorescent light. I twist around, shielding my eyes from the radiant glare off a white linoleum floor. A million crickets chirp through the buzzing bulbs.

I stand motionless and disoriented when a glimmer of movement appears. A small figure scurries out of sight. *What could that be now?* With my eyes now accustomed to the barrage of light, beaten into submission, a door closes softly to the left. I approach the area and read "Supply Room." *Is this where that thing came from? Maybe it was someone who can help get me out of this place. I must hurry and find them!*

With bare feet against the squeaky clean, bright white floor, I begin to jog, picking up speed like a jet rumbling down the dotted-line runway. While running through the corridors, I notice this area is polar opposite of the previous location. There are no other doors to be found here, just colorless, barren walls that abruptly end in ninety-degree angles. The maze-like passageways resemble a hospital. *But where are the people—and the rooms?*

I'm running faster than I ever have, whipping around the corners with ease, turning on a dime and giving change back. My feet hardly feel the need to contact the floor except to spring my weightless body into the air once again. If I didn't know any better, I'd swear I'm running 100 miles an hour. The blank walls are wrapped in a blur as a realization occurs: stopping from a dead sprint at this speed will yank my concealed bones outside the skin.

Cutting the next corner, I see the spark of movement once again, only much closer. *I'm gaining on it.* Feeling that whatever is ahead is within my grasp, I sprint even harder. I dart around the next corner, and I'm presented a better view. *A boy.*

*I'm coming, kid. There's no telling what's going to happen when I catch you, but rest assured, I will.*

My long legs make short work of his adolescent stature. While on a long straightaway, I can discern the young boy has a shimmering object clutched in one hand. He senses me coming. I would scream to him if I had any breath to spare.

Twenty yards away, the kid stops and disappears to the right. I gradually slow down to avoid breaking an ankle as the first door since the supply room appears. I stand, panting, with my hands intertwined above my head, permitting my lungs to expand, ballooning my heaving chest. A white sign with blue lettering reads, "JANITORIAL CLOSET." I grab and push the silver handle, swinging the door open.

Blood is spraying in every conceivable direction like a summertime sprinkler buried in a matted-down grassy puddle. The little boy's wrist is shooting red spatter, painting cardboard boxes a cabernet red, creating cascading waterfalls of bodily fluid in a stack of bed pans, where they fill up one by one, imitating ice cube trays.

The child is slashing away at his own left wrist with a medical bone saw like a person possessed.

I stand in the doorway, stunned. The boy doesn't acknowledge my presence or break focus from his work. He simply drags the saw back and forth, back and forth. The unforgiving teeth tear through the soft pink muscle and rubbery blue veins.

Chewing.

Grinding.

"What the *hell* are you doing?" I lunge toward the child, slipping on the blood-soaked floor, and collapse beside him. I rip the saw from the boy's hand mid-stroke, prying it from between the pinched bone, and toss the sticky tool underneath a huge set of storage shelves. Frothy blood wraps his arm in red lace.

*The bleeding hasn't stopped. I need to stop the bleeding.* If ever there was a time for a tourniquet, this would be it. I don't have a belt, and a frantic search around the room reveals only a pile of used cleaning rags. My trembling fingers snatch the rags with one hand and the child's now limp, hinged wrist with the other. I attempt to elevate the cold, dangling wrist, pressing the handful of cloth into the mangled flesh. I know I need to apply more pressure, but it is so delicate, barely hanging on by a thread.

Looking up from the chemical-stained rags that are beginning to soak through, I meet the eyes of the child for the first time. These are not grateful eyes; these are hateful eyes.

"You didn't let me finish."

"Why would you do this to yourself?" I stammer through anxious breaths.

"I knew you'd try to stop me. You always do," the boy remotely replies.

"We have to find you a doctor. Thank God we're in a hospital."

The child smirks as his blood warms my palms.

*I have to save this kid.*

"What on earth is leaking out from under *this* door?" I'm startled to hear from the other side. The door swings inward as I reach out to carry the child. A towering, thin man in a long, white lab coat is revealed. He is so unnaturally tall that his paper-white hair is flattened by the doorframe.

His cadaverous skin is the texture of salt-weathered wood from an abandoned ocean pier.

He inquires, "Can someone *please* explain to me why there is a *mess* in my ward? You *people* must have forgotten what transpired the last time someone forgot to tidy up." He folds his lanky arms, cupping his palms around each pointed elbow.

25

I'm kneeling on the bloody floor, cradling the child's nearly severed limb, noticing the man doesn't seem to mind standing in the blood. Seeing my puzzlement, he says, "Not to worry, the janitor has a *fascinating* way of cleaning up filth." He turns, spinning on the ball of his dress shoe and snaps his long white coat. He begins to walk briskly down the hallway, leaving a crude trail of red boot prints on the once pristine floor.

No matter how insane this may be, that man is our last chance. I lift the child's flimsy body and sprint after the bloody trail. "Help, doctor! Please! Don't go! Can't you see this boy needs you?"

He continues to walk.

"You bastard! What is the *matter* with you?" I scream.

The lanky man continues with his coat flaps swaying with every bloody step.

Through tears, I proclaim, "He has so much to live for!" The man pauses and turns to face me in the center of the hall.

Approaching him with the child nestled in my arms, he asks, "Why? Why should the child live when he so clearly wishes to die?"

"He doesn't *know* what he wants, but I'm certain he doesn't want *this!*"

Glancing down at the boy's mutilated wrist, the man cocks his creased brow line and replies in a flat tone, "I believe you are mistaken."

With tears streaming down my cheeks, I declare, "No,

I'm *not*. This kid is supposed to grow up strong, fall in love, have children, and die an old, happy man. *You* cannot take that away from him."

"Hand me the child and go," the doctor says.

"What? I'm going with you. I have to make sure he's all right—"

"You already have. Now go. You mustn't be here any longer. I cannot help him while you are here. Leave, while we still have time."

Feeling uncertain, but out of options, I decide to hand the child over to the tall man. The doctor embraces the boy against his colossal torso and repeats, "Go."

I walk backwards, shuffling away from the pair but never looking away. Once I'm thirty feet back, the man turns counterclockwise and proceeds down the long corridor, vanishing around a corner.

*He's going to be all right. I think I made the right decision. What other choice did I have?*

## 4

I turn to notice I'm approaching the janitor's closet again. A shadow defiles the silence. *Somebody is in there.*

Looking in the room as I walk past, a uniformed man is inside. His hair is so red it appears to have caught fire. His unkempt, bushy eyebrows are stolen from a backwoods owl, horned, full of untrustworthy expression. Within his spotted hands, he grips a long-handled mop, pushing it back and forth as the blood smears across the floor. The congealing plasma makes a discernible SMACK as he lifts and drops the mop, all accompanied by the jingling keys against his boney hip.

He looks up and leans his body against the long handle, saying with a snarling grin, "Lotta juice for a little kid. I've been waiting to find out how much you've got, Ard." His menacing eyes travel up and down my body; a singular front tooth chews on his lower lip.

*How does he know my name? Is any of this real?*

"It's real, Ard. More real than anything in your pathetic life. But tonight's the night. I'm gonna peel you like a fucking onion. Layer by layer. Each stinkin' more than the last."

Our silent, violent stares meet as instant enemies.

He leans the mop against the nearest wall with such care it barely registers a noise, even in our hushed state. The janitor, in his well-starched, crisp uniform with light stitching reading, *Maynard,* reaches toward the storage cabinet. His curly-haired, pale fingers lift the top blood-filled bedpan. His hooked nails, each the color of a heavily used cigarette filter, tap the metal. The pan's contents shift within, a small stormy ocean residing in its shiny curves.

*What is he doing?*

While holding the pan with both hands in front of his chest, his raspy voice croons, "Ya' know, I should be thanking you for saving that little twat... job security." The container turns upward; thick blood falls to the floor in a perfect, red stream. The liquid splashes onto the pink-smeared floor. While focused on my eyes, the janitor moves the pan in a slow but calculated motion. Breaking my own stare and glancing toward his feet, I see he has drawn an obvious lowercase *t* onto the linoleum below.

I am rooted, mesmerized.

When he finishes, the man places the silver pan back atop the stack. The janitor grabs a handful of pant leg in each palm, hiking up his tight-fitted trousers. Now equipped with a greater range of motion, he squats toward his creation. The man positions himself onto all fours, above the grotesque depiction.

My once hardened, intimidating stare has crumbled away, leaving only the ruins of fractured horror.

"Death is her name and she's hungry." His voice gargles as a death rattle, commencing the countdown of my final moments. Signaling the end is near. The janitor leans close to the portrayal and inhales deep through his flared nostrils. "Death is her name and she's *coming*."

Inhaling purity, exhaling putridity.

After a moment's pause, he breathes with a smile. "I *love* my job." His mouth opens, unleashing an abnormally wide, chalky tongue. Lowering further toward the ground, he drags his tongue through the workings of the sketch, tracing the long portion with the flaccid organ.

Standing at my angle, it appears as a regular *t* or cross symbol.

But to him, it is upside down.

His nose is an upended arrow pointing toward a brash, sinister smile as he devours the downward-facing cross, savoring its existence. The creator and the destroyer. The life-giving liquid transforms his white tongue into a scalding hot red. I witness its rejuvenation. With each second, the tongue awakens more, flinching and jumping in sporadic bursts.

When he has completed the length of the drawing, the tongue reels back behind his smirking lips. His hair crackles and sears, now composed of burning coals that hiss with the cries of a million doomed souls. The scent of a campfire fills my nostrils—but not a fire where one would roast marshmallows or blacken hot dogs with charcoal. This is the scent that's born when flesh meets flame. The aroma of scorched hair and yellow fat fills the air as it pops like strips of thick cut bacon on a rusty pan.

Lifting his head, the janitor licks his lips, applying a thin coat of ruby lipstick. "Death is her name and she's here to stay." The skin of his face is stretched tightly, shrink-wrapping his harsh features. Every peak and valley of his skull is highlighted and contoured. His eyes are holes in his head, floating at the bottom of a murky cauldron. He is a crevasse in the shape of a man. His internal void tugs at my soul with the gravitational pull of a black hole. An entity as old as time itself. A being that must feed to survive.

Gleaming upwards through his peaked eyebrows, his glassy, party-horn tongue unrolls from his mouth, devouring the lateral portion of the disappearing depiction.

*What will happen once he's finished? My toes are approaching the chasm, and the world is shifting– pulling me in.*

Without another moment's hesitation, I sprint away from the demented man, back down the hall from which I came.

His guttural, cackling laughter follows.

<u>5</u>

Loudspeakers scream, voices shriek, vocal cords howl. Each sound originating from inside the walls.

Tucked in like a frightened child, concealed like a dirty secret.

They must be everywhere, because there is never a break in the sound, never even a momentary lull that leads one into the next. Constant, blaring, unrelenting surround sound where a single, dominant voice cuts through the chatter. "Death is her name and she's *hungry!*" The noise vacuums the air from the hall, suffocating sound. "Death is her name and she's coming to town!"

A thousand roaring tea kettles.

My body sprints with the speed and agility of a world-class athlete. Legs driving, arms pumping, my stationary head adorned with a peeled grin, elastic lips and cheeks rolling to the back of my neck, left behind if not attached.

Still, I feel the janitor's seething breath there, hot with corruption, just below my prickly hairline. His spittle saturates my collar as his red-hot tongue lops the sweat beads off my flapping earlobe. His pointed chin rests against the crest of my shoulder as he screams— fiendish screeching, hellish wailing. His crimson face bobbling, his mechanical jaws chomping with the force of a hydraulic press. His bulging, bloodshot eyes belong in a circus sideshow. His mouth is wrapped around my ear, his white lips sealed tight, force-feeding me every scrap of sound. Each syllable laced with halitosis and decay, every bit made especially for me. The air he breathes is heavy, weighted with the world's capacity for malice, lust, and self-hatred.

I cannot escape his pace. I cannot escape *him.*

I'm a fly in a trap—helpless, pathetic, thrashing inside a dew-dropped web. All is dark, all is wrong. Not seeing, but *feeling* the predator approaching nearer. Dreaded, stomach-churning anticipation. Its marbled eyes glistening with ravenous opportunity. My pygmy wings struggle and push to separate from this eternal glue. The tiny water beads fling about, their chaotic soaring broadcasting the inner panic. A deranged child sprints on a train track; a thousand barbed legs flicker across the silk strands. The deadly excitement lubricates its jaws as I stand at the end of its tunnel vision. The beast never squanders a morsel; nothing goes to waste. I can find some comfort there.

*Lie still, don't fight, it will be over in a second. Give in, accept fate. Easy enough to say until the daggers sink into my skin.*

"Death is her name, come to harvest your pain."

*I need to stop.* I've been running full-speed for God knows how long and have nothing left. I haven't passed a single door, window, or even a nail hole since that nightmarish closet. Only the sound to keep me company.

Slowing down to a jog, I glance behind, surprised and relieved to find the devilish janitor is nowhere to be seen. I don't think he came after me at all. *I could have sworn he was* attached *to me...*

Maybe he doesn't need to chase me because there seems to be no way out. He knows I'll have to go back or starve. He'll just be there, *waiting* with his dry, white tongue. *Thirsty.*

*I'll stop around the next corner.*

"Death is her name, retreat as you may, there is no escape."

I sling around the ninety-degree corner, pinning myself against the empty wall.

The sound stops.

My mind exhales a combined sigh of relief and suspicion. While attempting to catch my breath, my head pokes beyond the previous corner. *He'll be there, staring into my eyes as our noses graze. I'm sure of it.* My breath pauses as I peek around, conserving the oxygen for one last, helpless scream.

But he is not there. No one is coming. I chuckle a nervous brew of nauseous joy and shivering elation.

*Man, I'm such a pansy, always running away or hiding underneath my covers at the first sign of danger. I should've gone apeshit on that redheaded bastard and shown him who's really psycho. Yeah, maybe I'll do that.* I'll walk right up to him and say, "Don't mess with me, broom boy, or I'll shove that thing so far up your ass you'll be walking around like a Popsicle!"

But first, I need to rest, if only for a moment.

Everything is so unclear, so incredibly beyond my reasoning. Unexplained, like how a single tune of a song can transport a person back into the moment it impacted their life. The deep-seeded memory forgotten, enshrouded in the eons before the first chord is struck. But then all the sights, sounds, scents, and sensations are conjured from thin air. Just as authentic as the moment it occurred, shockingly real.

With my knees bending forward, my sweat-soaked back slides down the wall until I'm seated on the tile floor. My blood-crusted feet stand walleyed as the Achilles tendons flatten against the cold ground. *Oh man, I never would've thought linoleum could be so damn comfortable.*

This has been the longest, scariest, and strangest night of my life. I'm well past the point of stressed, and the word *confusion* doesn't scratch the surface. I'll rest my eyes for a couple minutes; that will help make sense of all this.

Taking one last glance around the corner, the coast is clear, and I let go.

## 6

I *hear music.* I force my crust-stuck eyelids open and await clarity through the foggy haze of sleep. It doesn't take long to decipher that this is *not* the hallway where I fell asleep. I find myself seated on a hard, stone floor with my back leaned against a flaky, stucco-textured wall. My palms press against the rough rock, elevating me from the floor where I stand inside a great, circular chamber. My murky eyes trace the deliberate, inlaid pattern of the stone beneath my feet. The unforgiving kernels display a contrast of black on white, where the black portion swirls around the room. I somehow *know* it forms a giant spiral. Its curvatures wind about the floor, pinpoint-thin at the center while expanding at each meandering bend. It seems never-ending.

At its center is a white grand piano. The instrument is draped with a thick, flowing linen, and an elegant player's bench is seated behind the keys where each clawed foot grapples a purple glass marble. Above the piano is a marvelous, three-tiered crystal chandelier affixed with dozens of burning candles. The crystal globes hang in clusters, the pull of gravity gradually transforming their spherical shape into tear drops. The chandelier is fastened into a dramatic, cove ceiling with a dainty, looped gold chain.

The ceiling's smooth edges are adorned with familiar depictions. Each image is real enough to touch, to remember, yet blurring with each breath I take. I swear I see myself up there, a painstakingly accurate representation, but the more I attempt to focus my eyes, the more the figures become blurred blobs of decomposing paint.

The candlelight casts an orange glow, illuminating the textured walls in a flickering golden hue. With my vision craned to the ceiling, a fat glob of liquid wax careens toward the piano from a lopsided candle. Its descension disappears against the instrument.

*That's not linen at all—that's wax.*

My slatted eyes expand as I realize the piano is *covered* with long, dried icicles formed around the instrument's edges, each flowing to the stone beneath, draped like a frozen waterfall. Thick beads resembling witch's warts decorate every peculiar inch. That amount of accumulation must've taken years. *How long has this piano been here?*

The piano continues playing, turning a blind eye to my presence. There doesn't appear to be anything else in this room—no furniture, no people. Nothing but the piano and its steadfast music. The white and black keys are mechanically elevated and depressed, crafting the most unsettling melody imaginable. A ballad never meant for living ears; music suited only for the road to the underworld. The somber tune accentuates the lack of hope, the pain of regret, and the unwavering promise of eternal despair.

*Who'd program a self-playing piano to perform such a grim ballad?* Needless to say, I don't care for its tone. "Do you take requests?" I ask through a rhetoric filter.

*Silence.*

SLAM! The playing ceases as the key cover throws itself shut with unnecessary force. *That is an unexpected feature.* The wooden player's stool backs away from the keys, causing a staggered *screeeeech* against the bumpy stones. The glass marbles chip, leaving glass shavings against the stone.

Clop, clop, clop.

Invisible, hard-soled shoes reverberate off the stony floor.

SCREEEEECH!

The padded stool is slammed against the underside of the piano, landing cockeyed beneath the ivory keys. *This is no self-playing piano.*

I creep backward, moving away from the source. Clop, clop, clop. The sound follows me. I circle around the great room, finding nowhere to go—no exits, no hiding places, and no weapons. I tread faster, trying to gain some separation from the sound. Despite the effort, I can *feel* it right in front of me, no matter how fast I go.

Looking toward the curved walls, my glimmering shadow retreats from an invisible foe. A thick layer of sweat cakes my forehead while searching for any way out of this latest dose of torture. I must've circled the room three times and still nothing. *How could there be no entryways? This piano must have been placed in here somehow. Who's been changing out all those candles?* I feel the urge to lie on my back, untie my bladder, and surrender like a petrified dog.

*I can't keep doing this. I regret not confronting that psychotic janitor, and now I'm running from something I can't even see! No more.*

I stop. The sound also stops.

A body of coldness emanates in the space before me. Dark, brooding, malevolent.

I throw a Hail Mary right hook, equipped with greater force than when I punched the solid motel door, except this time impacting nothing but wintry air as the momentum spins me 180 degrees.

"Show yourself, you f—"

*My windpipe. I can't breathe.*

My esophagus constricts with such intensity that my throat desires to split in two. I gasp for oxygen, attempting to break the hold of whatever is around my throat. My desperate hands find only my own skin, the grip tightening as the desperation grows. I begin clawing away at my own Adam's apple like a deranged animal, my fingernails digging into the spongy tissue. My hard nails become so packed with meat they are rendered dull. The warmth of fresh blood gushes down my chest. My eyes overflow with blurring water as they feel determined to explode from their socket housing.

*This is it. No one is coming to help. I guess this is how I'm going to die. But what if there is nothing after death? Just nothing. No heaven, no hell, not even reincarnation.* That premise is even more terrifying than an eternity in the underworld; at least hell is *something. How does it feel to not exist? I don't remember before I was conceived. I'm not ready, but I'm going. Ready to re-learn what I've forgotten.*

The room is narrowing. The corners of my vision pulsate, closing more with every sorrowful beat of my suffocating heart. As my final breath exhales, I accept this predicament. I embrace this fate.

My knees buckle, the rounded caps collapsing onto the jagged, rocky surface.

I suck in every scrap of air that will fit into my depleted lungs. I can breathe.

*It let me go. But why?*

Looking toward the piano through tear-shrouded eyes, I inhale with more gratitude than ever before. For the first time, *acknowledging* the precious oxygen filling my lungs, giving me life.

Clop, clop, clop.

The sound moves toward the center of the room where the tufted bench is gently slid from underneath the massive instrument. The key lid opens, and its dry hinges exhale a soft groan as the cover rests lightly against the carved backdrop. A single key is played, then another. The same dark melody commences, and with every note struck, a single drop of wax falls toward the piano.

*First this thing is trying to kill me, and now it's just going to play that same horrid song?*

**OOOOMMMM!**

Eight keys are simultaneously pressed, sending a sudden gush of wax barreling down, adding a wet sliver to the mountain of melted candles. The black inlaid stones that form the floor's spiral begin to drop, each one a little farther than the one before, crafting a downward spiraling staircase.

*Is it allowing me to leave or leading me to further misery?*

My body stands over its feet as I realize this may be the only way out.

Without an option, I descend the circular steps.

My lacerated feet stagger down the bumpy stones, the scored soles riddled with abrasions, peeled flesh, and translucent blisters. The pain is present but not altogether unpleasant. A *loose tooth* type of discomfort; like when your jaw clenches against the ailment, the pinch of its soreness sending dull flashes through your bones. Upon release, its flat pain throbs throughout your cells, instilling the strange desire to repeat.

Looking upward as my head becomes level with the floor, the room's walls are *melting*, imitating the dripping candles. Huge wax clumps speed in tracks down the once spotless surface.

The chandelier's numerous candles roar with intensity. A suspended wildfire. The jade flames dance about, filling the room with blinding color. The overwhelming heat from the jagged flames melts the fixture's support chains, sending it crashing onto the piano below.

Decades, centuries of hardened wax as big as icebergs soar throughout the great room.

It all happens in an instant. The white piano blazes a

bright, scorching orange. Colossal, pointed flames whirl around the instrument as the melody speeds and becomes more pronounced. The fallen chandelier is perched as a mangled crown. A tornado of wind and blistering heat swells within the room, sending sharp shockwaves against my clawed throat.

The flames consume everything in their path. Flickers of molten matter soar through the bulging, swollen clouds of tarnished silver smoke. A bulky chunk of ember lands atop the player stool, igniting its dry, tufted silk. The fire crawls in mid-air, *clawing* against logic, levitating above the stool's center.

The music accelerates, now unrecognizable.

The blaze begins to create shapes, a *form* upon the player's chair. The flames slither upward, drawing the silhouette of a person—a man on fire. He shifts and sways with the breakneck tempo of the impossible melody. His fiery fingers prance on the charcoaled keys as the simmering flames trace and scorch his non-existent flesh.

This spectacle is hypnotic, yet I cannot stay. The ever-expanding flames are devouring every morsel of oxygen. Coughing with each breath, my scrunched, wet eyes attempt to see through the thick smoke. Squinting against the flames, my vision is sharpened to a point. Breathing in the smell of sulfur, the taste of smoldering ivory. *The room has found another way to choke me.*

The whipping wind sends pond ripples through my cheeks and, for an instant, clears the blanketed smoke. I see movement up there, figures in motion against the bowed ceiling. It *is* me in the picture, cradled inside a dark hole, studying something in my hands. The scene washes away. Now I see a flurry of movement into a crowded street. I'm in the center, lying still—

The vision abruptly ends as the mini-atmosphere returns to overcast, the clouds reclaiming their rightful property.

The ferocious heat and accompanying wind have become unbearable, the forceful combination extracting the moisture from my pores, the lines of my forehead deepening with each passing second. Its thousand fingertips toss, comb, and tug the hair from my scalp. If I stay here any longer, my face will soon mimic the candles—the melted skin separating from the skull, dripping off my exposed jawline in hairy, shower-drain clumps—unmasking the original me. The flames will tongue the bone, taking bets on how many licks it takes to get to the marrow.

*I'm leaving.* With a final glance at the mesmerizing scene, the blazing man turns his head to the right, rendering a slight nod in my direction. The gesture causes the top half of his burning head to detach. The incendiary skull shatters into red confetti and gray ash on its impact against the stones. His body begins disintegrating in the gale; embers peel from his shoulders and legs like cigarette sparks from a moonlit joyride. He is disappearing, but not before I'm overcome by a sense of odd familiarity.

I run down the stone steps, my body winding around the most ancient of all symbols. Gliding along its immortality, its perseverance, its mystery. Spinning, corkscrewing into the center of the Earth.

Becoming one with the spiral.

Dingy cobwebs round the corner of each step. The dormant webs stand abandoned, yet the structures remain. My feet stomp past the abandoned homes of countless generations of ghost spiders, the children never branching off far from their thin-legged parents. My feet press and spring off the soft strings. The webs tug at my ankles, their sole purpose to ensnare prey. But try as they might, all the strength has left their grip.

The light dims a shade with each flash of my eyelids. Every movement leads me farther and deeper beneath the great room where desolate darkness engulfs the searing flames.

A thick, crocheted blanket of bitter coldness embraces me. The frigid moisture clings to the air, its chill gnawing at each bone, winding each tendon, and shoving needles into my nostrils. The type of cold that crudely reawakens decade-old injuries, summoned from their lengthy slumber, making every movement sluggish, sedated, and frail. The floating, white-gloved hands of an astronaut.

The blackness has swallowed me. Even looking upwards to the former inferno, the entire world is obscured. With both hands pressed along the opposing sides of the spiral staircase, I balance myself, hoping each step isn't the last. *Okay, stay calm. Keep taking steps. This must lead somewhere just like every other insane obstacle has.*

Stone step, stone step, *none*—

My eager foot struggles to find the needed support yet

comes up empty. My body lurches forward, twisting and struggling to force itself back onto the previous step. My fingernails drag along the smooth rock walls, dislodging the throat skin buried underneath.

I'm falling.

Weightlessness—what I imagine one encounters in the deep vacuum of space—is now my reality. I scream but hear only silence.

Am I falling or *floating?*

Either way, my internal organs now reside within my palate, and I'm positive they could be seen on the tip of my tongue.

## 7

I never dreamed that darkness could be *this* dark. It's as if light has never touched this place. Time has forsaken me as I've been here floating, motionless.

*Have I fallen into an isolation tank? A specially designed sensory deprivation tank. Is this all an experiment gone wrong? A drug-induced test with my mind feeding data to a supercomputer through countless rainbow wires? That is the only explanation for this place.*

I continue looking in every bleak direction in hopes of seeing something, anything—the blink of a comet streaking through eternity, the multi-colored blaze of its endless tail scarring the sky, or perhaps the white moon positioned as a vacant straw hole as I sit at the bottom of an empty cup. Yet, nothing. The foundation of my sanity is eroding, slipping with each hollow moment.

*Have I gone blind?*

The feeling of being an autumn leaf comes to mind—its once emerald green, flourished self now decayed into a dusty brown. Its former, flexible points hardened into a delicate, crackling shell. It holds onto the past, weathering a thousand breezes, holding tight. So absolute of its place in the world until that final gust of air comes surging from another world. It can be heard rumbling in the distance, gaining strength, howling like an oncoming freight train, an unstoppable force barreling toward the only home the leaf has ever known.

You'd batten down the hatches if you had time. You'd repair the shingles if you had the energy. But you're tired—oh so tired—of holding onto an untrue reality, gripping onto the hope of brighter days that will never come. Its carnal blow beats against the underside of your being, an uppercut into the withered soul. You try to hold on, but it is too much. The combination of its insatiable strength versus the lack of your own causes the choice to be easy.

Detached. Soaring.

Every concealed bird nest tucked inside the branches is now exposed without your protection. Abandoned, left behind, next on the squall's kill list. Your pointed edges cartwheel through the air at the mercy of its winded highways without a map—off to die where kitchen cleaning products shop for perfume and the trees stand as seasonal corpses in the forest. The dead of winter exposing the ugliness that the spring conceals.

It is liberating, terrifying, but it is done. I've lost what little control I once possessed.

Although the world has been taken away, the memories inside my mind have not. My brain begins to replace the missing sights and sounds of the present with those of my past, every memory that the fear and confusion has masked since the motel room.

They fill the void with color, with hope, with heartbreak.

# PART II

# FRAGMENTS OF THE PAST

## Ten Years Prior

### 1

I never believed my parents when they warned me about how life changes as you grow up. Telling me that friends, girlfriends, and all these people you cannot fathom living without will become small frames residing within your deep memory.

"You'll find out for yourself one day. I wasn't *always* an old lady, you know," my mother would say across the dinner table, the fumes from her fresh perm injected into each bite of food. "You need to be your own man, independent. Don't ever lean on anybody, because you're apt to fall over."

My mother has always been the light of my world, and she was right. After high school, my *friends* dropped like flies during an unanticipated spring freeze. These days, I notice familiar faces in the crowd, combinations of features that shared so many fond memories, but now I can't even recall their names. A subtle nod and a confused glance is all that remains of a pivotal adolescent relationship. Fragments from the past.

My knees bend, transforming my shape to fit onto the couch as I continue to recount my own existence.

I was on top of the world in my senior year, but following graduation, I was no longer a shark at the top of the food chain. Just another clueless 18-year-old burnout, now that nobody was holding my hand. My new plankton existence. I opted to take some time to figure it all out, but as I bounced from one miserable job to another, the years flew by and so did my youth.

With each passing day, I discovered that it's easy to make new friends but difficult to keep them. I don't have many friends anymore. The smart ones left town to make something of themselves, and the others remain glued to their teenage years. I don't seem to fit in with either, so I keep myself company most days. Life is much simpler being alone, but I must admit something is missing.

I've existed on this earth for over twenty years, and yet I know nothing about myself. I have no idea what I'm capable of, what strengths I possess, or my place in this world. I want to be tested. Each day, as I steer through unmarked back roads, my thoughts wander into the starless corners of my mind. A dark place where tragedy is welcomed at any moment.

Perhaps a squealing-tire joyride transforming into catastrophe. The music blaring and crackling the cheap speakers, the cigarette ash launching fireworks out of the side window, the thousand trees behaving as stagnant pedestrians with nowhere to go. There are no guardrails on these roads, no warning signs of dangerous turns, no notice of the inebriated driver straddling the non-existent median, and no indication of the family of sprinting deer. As I trail these vehicles, I can't help but wish something would happen. Something tragic. Something unforeseen.

Ahead, the maroon sedan takes the curve with too much confidence. The brake pedal is neglected as the under-inflated tire attempts to hold on, to obey its master, but it's too much pressure. It is just too much.

The rubber explodes in a rifle blast, the stale, years-old oxygen releases from its dark, rubber prison, returning to its natural habitat. Its molecules warped and deformed from eons of abuse. Deflation, inflation, and confinement.

The car pivots to the right–vertical one second, horizontal the next. The left wheels buckle, grinding to a halt. The sedan takes flight, twirling and rolling as it cuts through the wind, a vehicular gymnast. The blown out tires and gray underbody face the clouds, then the road, and repeat. It's as if gravity has lost its grip on this one piece of the world. It is free. A scattered bundle of blonde hair trails the blue sky and hugs the car roof. Every part, every drop of fuel, every person is at the uncaring will of inertia. It lands, roof first. The sparks flying against the pavement are beautiful, but the sound is not. The paint layers disintegrate as the asphalt chews the metal into smaller bites. The slide continues until the laws of motion have had their fill, leaving a breadcrumb trail of glass, fast food wrappers, and plastic hubcaps.

My tires screech, a chunk of cracked bumper lodging in the rear axle. I exit the car, running toward the carnage, into the flames, toward the screams. The first on scene, their fates are in my hands—a complete stranger, yet now the most important person in their world. Becoming a part of something bigger than myself—a hero—if only for a day. Although I'm there to help, their sacrifice is my gain. I would learn more about myself in those eternal seconds than I have in my entire life.

*Who am I kidding? If that ever happened, which I*

*half-hope it doesn't, I would only disappoint those inside and myself.*

But tonight is no different from any other night. There are no heroic moments, no flying cars. I look over at the empty, neighboring couch cushion, picturing my beautiful wife seated there. I watch the ghost of myself walking barefoot across the carpet, carrying an ice-cream-filled coffee mug as she's cocooned in her favorite blanket, tonight's occasion seeming so insignificant, yet further strengthening our bond. The small moments bind our souls together, each of us content to just *be* with one another. Finding everything I need in that person: a lover and a best friend.

Despite these desires, I am alone and have been for some time. It's hard to remember how long it has been since I shared myself with someone. The empty days are grueling, but not compared to the nights.

I hate sleeping in an empty bed. I dread crawling beneath the covers each night, forced to face the painful admission of another day without finding someone. The utter failure. *Is it me?* It must be, but I'm uncertain why. So much time has passed; concepts that once came easy now appear alien.

*How do you allow yourself to be loved?*

The whole notion seems more awkward and unnatural with each barren day.

<u>2</u>

Last week, I interviewed for a new job—a carpenter's apprentice. The interview went surprisingly well. The owner, Dusty, seemed to like me for *some* reason.

"Do you have any construction or handyman experience?" he asked with a mouthful of dark tobacco, his lower lip swollen and jutting out like the remnants of a savage bar fight.

"Besides working at the plant—I'll be honest—I don't." That was a painful admission, considering I'm twenty-three years old. But I can't hide my inability if I start working here.

"Hmmm. Well, gotta start someplace. I sure wasn't an expert the first time I spun a drill, but here I am offering you a job."

"You'll hire me?"

He shrugs his plaid shoulders. "Sure, you seem like a good kid, and don't worry, we'll show you the ropes."

I couldn't believe he was willing to take a chance on me. I applied as a last ditch effort after being laid off at the paper mill. I'd been with the company for less than a year, and the old saying rang true as the personnel cuts began: *last ones in, first ones out.*

I was upset about the firing but even more agitated that I didn't get the chance to quit first. I hated that job, despised each minute of every endless shift. My entire life, I've heard people complain about the paper mill stench—myself included—but that odor is *nothing* compared to being inside the factory. Cooked sulphur. I never ate before, during, and *rarely* after a shift, because I knew it would come right back up. Most workers and nearby residents were accustomed to the smell. I couldn't decide whether to feel sorry or envious of them.

I don't know why I stayed until the end. I should've left that place long ago, never imagining I'd be fired from the worst job I'd ever had. Like the countless logs during my tenure, my ego's been fed through a shredder, as I'm not even good enough to do something I loathe.

But today is my first day on Dusty's crew. I didn't get much sleep last night as I stayed up late watching countless construction tutorials on my glaring, blue-tinted screen. I'm on a team of three men, including Dusty as the lead. The two guys said their names when we were introduced, but I was so nervous that I didn't hear a thing. Each is equipped with far more experience. This was apparent the moment I shook their hands, their firm grips riddled with hard calluses and flesh-colored bandages.

We load up into a four-door pickup truck. I sit in the backseat with an elbow rested upon a black toolbox and my boots on scattered sawdust. An old-fashioned musician hums through the speakers, the sincerity of his tone pacifying the passengers. I stare out the window as the waking world speeds by, focusing my eyes to slow it for a moment. The cab's air circulates the scents of sugary coffee and charred wood.

I hate first days, especially when you have no idea what you're doing *and* there's an audience. I do my best to remain confident, but beneath the tranquil exterior lies a petrified little boy. A swarm of anxiety creeps into my throat–this is the root of nightmares.

The truck stops alongside the curb of a peaked, red-brick home. The men open their doors, each swallowing a final sip of coffee before stepping onto the pavement with an exaggerated sigh. The two-storied house is beautiful with its lemon-yellow shutters and large wrap-around porch.

I begin helping the men unload the truck, eagerly grabbing the massive toolbox from the backseat. The younger guys exchange glances after watching me; their eyebrows raise as a chuckle falls from their lips. I carry the heavy box toward the porch, nearly spilling it in the grass as its rusted flakes fall like snow.

"We won't be needing that for this job, Arden. I should've told you. Thanks though," Dusty says from behind. My wobbling legs and faltering arms return the massive box to the truck, the internal metal tools clanking within. My two coworkers pass me on the grass, not offering to help as they pretend to be occupied. Their cut-off shirts waft unwashed underarm stench into my open, gasping mouth. I heave the box into the backseat, and already, I'm tired and discouraged.

*What am I doing here?*

"Think we've got all we need; follow me." Dusty digs his thumb and forefinger inside his lip and flings a charcoal lump onto the curb.

Dusty and I walk the path to the house and ascend the stairs. He leads us to the porch's corner and points a stubby finger at a small area. Three boards are sunken in, cracked, and warped.

"This one's pretty straightforward, boys. Let's get these bad boards out and throw some fresh ones in. The lady of the house is a family friend, so let's make sure to do our best. Arden, I'm gonna give you the lead."

"Okay, sure thing." This is bad.

I remove the damaged boards, prying out the twisted, rust-caked nails with little difficulty. My empty head fills with false self-confidence. After a quick safety run-through on the miter saw, I'm ready to size and cut the fresh boards. The pieces need to be angled on both sides. On top of that, all three wood slabs are angled differently. The original installer hadn't been a perfectionist, but luckily for this old lady, Dusty is.

The scrap pieces pile up as I angle too sharp, cut too short, and even angle the wrong direction. The snickering of my new coworkers fills my ears as I wonder if I belong here at all. Dusty places his weathered hand on my sweat-drenched back and says,

"Don't listen to those idiots. Their piles looked like mountains in comparison on their first days."

Feeling a bit better, I size and place two boards. On the final board, there remains a small, less than a half-inch gap between the angled wood and the baseboard. *Good enough. This lady won't care or even notice with her glaucoma-ridden eyes.*

"Do it over."

*You've got to be kidding.* My defeated expression says it all to my new boss.

Leaning down, he hands me another board. With his flat pencil tucked tight inside his cap, hanging over his right sideburn, he says, "If we're gonna do it, we're gonna do it right. If you decide to be something—if only for a day—be the best at it. That little, half-inch of extra effort is what separates the winners from the losers."

With splintered and blistered hands, I make the measurements once more. *Okay, the first angle still lines up perfectly, now onto the second.* Triple checking my pencil line in the wood, I decide on the location. Lining up on the saw, beads of sweat pour from my forehead to the sweltering porch below. The blade touches the wood twenty times before it spins.

The saw slices through the layers of compressed tree body. *Oh my God, did I go too far? Maybe not far enough so I can make another cut. I'm wasting everybody's time. I shouldn't be here! All these poor trees had to be chopped down, sawed, treated, and sold just for me to butcher them without purpose!*

Dusty interrupts my inner dilemma. "Well, go on. We'd like to get home sometime before the snowfall."

I walk over with my creation cradled tight in my arms, hovering above the final empty slat. I place the first end in and it's snug. Moving to the second angle, the stubborn board sits on top, jutting upward. A firm shove fails to aid it down further. It sticks out like a sore thumb.

*Oh my God, I must be the dumbest son of a bitch alive. Forget it, I'm quitting this job right now.*

While kneeling beside my failure, a shadow rises high above my head and moves down toward my fingers. Pulling my hands away, Dusty's tan, steel-toed boot comes slamming down on the board, seating it perfectly in position.

"Good angle," he says while pulling his cap off to wipe his brow, the forgotten pencil falling on the boards. "That one was more temperamental than a menopausal mother-in-law, I couldn't have done it better myself. But sometimes, you've got to *make* that thing fit."

*Kind of like me and this job.*

Regardless of how long it took or how embarrassed I became, this is one of the proudest moments of my life. No matter how badly I wanted to surrender, I didn't. And Dusty was right, it was all worth it in the end. It is one of those moments when I want to drop everything to call my mother, just to hear her say how proud she is.

Before this job, I'd never given this type of work much thought. Whenever I'd drive by a construction site and glance at the bearded, dirty men, I'd be filled with the notion that they were somehow beneath me. *How hard can it be to put up a house? Those hillbillies are doing it!* I was wrong again. The amount of math and science involved in even the smallest project surpasses any occupation I've ever had.

While on the job, Dusty always has me by his side, consistently exerting the extra effort to dumb things down to help me understand the craft. Regardless of whether he sees promise, or just enjoys teaching to keep his own skills sharp, I love it. The clean air is an added bonus.

I've now apprenticed for five months, each day becoming more proficient and requiring less supervision. I find myself anxious to wake up with the rising sun, if only to hang out with Dusty.

On this muggy July day, Dusty and I are putting the final touches on a deck we built onto a townhouse. It's nothing fancy, a square shaped 10' x 10' deck with three steps leading into the green grass of a fenced-in backyard. Nevertheless, I'm astonished to realize that I went from reading a saw's owner's manual a few months ago to affixing a permanent house structure in such a short time. As I'm bent down, searching for excess screws laying on the boards, the back door slides open.

Oddly enough, despite being here for three days, we haven't met the tenants. By now, I've grown accustomed to polite people offering refreshments or creepy customers opting to awkwardly watch us all day. My curiosity is piqued.

My gaze lifts and an angel is standing in the doorway. She looks through my soul as she says, "Great work." The simple words swim to my ears, singing a sweeter melody than any songwriter could hope to compose.

I am smitten, starstruck at the sight of her. My lips release an incoherent mumble.

I stand in slow motion, capturing every detail of her image from bottom to top. Brown, strappy sandals pave the way for a soft set of ankles. Smooth, tan skin leads to a pair of light green capris adorned with far too many pockets. The smallest sliver of skin is exposed between her curved hips and gray fitted tank top. Her flat stomach introduces her perfectly sized chest. A silky bundle of chocolate brown hair cascades down her left shoulder. Her protruding clavicle is restrained from leaping out by her thin shoulder strap. Her smooth neck supports a soft jawline, accentuating her facial features better than any master frame maker. Her face is too much for language to comprehend. The words to describe its perfection have yet to be conceived.

Standing now, our eyes lock. My mind is mesmerized by their deep aura. A pair of forest green supernovas stare back into me. I could be an astronomer gazing through a multi-million dollar telescope, discovering a vast, ancient secret of space.

The mysteries of the universe lie within her eyes.

"Didn't anyone teach you it's rude to stare?" she asks as the smallest hint of a flirtatious smile touches her lips.

*There's no way this girl would give me the time of day.* "Sorry, I didn't mean to stare. It's just I...couldn't force myself to look away."

She displays a curious expression as her left eyebrow arches upward, motioning toward a bobby pin in her hairline. I'm equally surprised of the words exiting my mouth.

The second chorus of our conversation begins. "Do you have any plans this Friday? I'm throwing a housewarming party. Would you like to christen the deck you've built?"

*If I had plans with the president, I'd cancel on his ass to make this party. Try to play it cool.*

"I think I could swing by. See you then." With a final perky smile and gracious spin, she's gone. *Perfect backside, too, by the way.*

I mock her dainty spin, twirling with my head in the clouds, oblivious to my surroundings. When I feather down, Dusty is standing with his thumbs tucked into the front of his tool belt, shaking his head with a chuckle on his lips.

"Never took you for the romantic type. Did she cast a spell on you? You're grinning like a half-wit with an ice cream cone!"

My cheeks redden, and my blissful mind can't think of anything clever to say.

Once I arrive home, I pace endlessly, trying to slow my thinking. "Okay, today is Thursday. The party is tomorrow—my God, that's a small window. What if she forgets about me and I creep her out? Was she inviting me out of courtesy? No, she went out of her way to include me, but why? Shit—SHITSHITSHIT! Did she tell me her name? Was I so dumbfounded and oblivious that I forgot to ask her freaking name? How do you show up to a party, knowing *one* person, but not even know their damn name? I can't go to this party. This is too much." I throw my arms in the air. Problem solved. Stress relieved.

As the stars appear, I barely sleep, tossing and turning through the dark.

## 3

This morning, my blank stare is directed out the passenger window as Dusty drives to a new job site. After five minutes on the road, he can no longer hold his tongue. "Ready for the wedding tonight?" he says with a tobacco-filled smirk.

"I'm not going."

"You're pulling my leg, right?" he mumbles, hawking a thick wad of blackness into a repurposed sweet tea container. I make a mental note *not* to drink sweet tea today.

"No, she doesn't want me there. She was just being nice," I reply as my head lowers.

His left hand tenses on the leather steering wheel as his opposite hand caresses the bare knuckle of his ring finger. "That may be the case, but you'll never know for certain unless you get your skinny ass there to find out! The last thing any woman wants is another guy who runs like a cheap pair of pantyhose."

"I don't even know her name, Dusty," I argue.

"Well, shit, let me look at the work order, numb nuts."

*Why didn't I think of that?* Dusty shuffles around with his clipboard, his denim knees steering the wheel, as tightness creeps up my spine.

"I don't think your little darling's name is Beatrice, do

you?" he asks as his hairless legs weave us through the pot-holed road. Dusty's bottom limbs were likely once covered in lush, dark hair. But through the years of hard work, the tiny curls have been rubbed, plucked, and torn away by rough denim and long socks, his body eventually submitting to the reality of his profession and all the odd physical quirks that come along with its paycheck. The only remaining bits of hair huddle around his moles like a winter campfire.

My eyes flick away from his legs, embarrassed that I may have been staring for a moment too long. "I have no idea, but I'd guess not."

Dusty dials a number on his phone.

" *Who* are you calling?" My voice is a wavering tone.

He simply glances in my direction.

"No. How obvious can you be, man?" I'm twelve years old again, immature beyond belief–my giggling friend telling my crush that I *like*, like her.

"Relax yourself. I'm gonna call and see if they're happy with the deck." As the phone rings, I'm doing my best to hide my quivering body.

The voicemail recites its rehearsed lines, and Dusty puts it on speakerphone. "Hello, you've reached the voicemail of Beatrice Bonneville. If you are a tenant in need of assistance, I'll be on vacation until next week and will return your call at my earliest convenience. Thank you."

This is not the angel's voice, and by the sound of it, this is an older lady who may become an *actual* angel in the near future. *Her landlord, thank God.*

Dusty shoots me a cocked eyebrow from the corner of his slanted eye, witnessing my relief. "Shit, I know you better than this old stick-shift pickup, don't I? I know how to make you purr, make you run as smooth as a baby's ass. But I also know how to grind your gears." He coughs a laugh into the windshield, the sun rays tracing each drop of spit as it sticks and glistens on the curved glass.

I can only shake my head as a fake laugh exits from behind my teeth, a puppet of myself.

The stars didn't align, meaning this must not be the right thing to do. At least that's how I justify my cowardice. Today has been one of those days where I'd rather stay at work than go home. At work I can hide from my problems and *pretend* to escape.

Making my reluctant entrance home, I plan on doing nothing but hiding in my own house. Bunkering down in the predictable security of my habitat—the one place in the world where I'm impenetrable. While crawling onto my barren sofa in my same old ratty pajamas, I feel ashamed to be me.

I sense the sickening regret my soul will suffer fifty years in the future for this decision. Will I be an old, unloved man, sitting in his cheap recliner that goes all the way flat, doubling as a pathetic bed, wondering: *What if I had done things differently?* The pocked, tender bedsores transforming the slightest movements into agony. This shell of a man is filled with the painful remorse of countless missed opportunities and doors forever closed, realizing there are no second go-arounds at life. Knowing that, although he may have lived a long time, he never truly *lived at all.* A shadow, a hermit, an ignored, abandoned soul in a hopeless nursing home without a friend to visit. He would be ready to die at that point, but the largest part of him will have passed on long ago. Maybe that time is tonight. Maybe tonight's decision will haunt my life with such intensity that its memory will banish me to my lonely hole in the earth.

Some people describe insanity as repeating the same motion but expecting a different result. How do I expect to find what I'm looking for if I don't have the guts to go get it? It won't fall into my lap as I rewatch this boring sitcom. With each potential opportunity passing, I think to myself: *There will be another in the future, and I'll take advantage of that one. Now is not the right time.*

Until there are no more chances and the well has run dry. I should have drunk from it before all the life-giving potential evaporated, the liquid absorbing into the clouds and falling into someone else's empty bucket. I hope they will be smarter than me.

Dusty's right. Why *wouldn't* I go to this party? What do I have to lose? Nothing. If it goes well, that's great. If it doesn't, all these people will return to being strangers once again. With my heart fluttering, I convince myself out the door.

Driving to the party, I've never experienced this type of overwhelming anxiousness coursing through my body. I finally feel awake. I feel alive.

Halfway to her house, my heart sinks in my chest when it occurs to me that I forgot to bring something. My mother's voice rings between my ears, "Never show up to a party empty-handed."

I jerk the steering wheel, pulling into a local grocery store with my rear wheels squealing. As I jog through the parking lot, a slew of confused looks beam toward me from these non-emergency shoppers who cannot comprehend my present amount of stress. My feet shuffle around the fluorescent-lighted market as I ponder the options: day-old oatmeal cookies, a semi-rotted fruit basket, happy birthday balloons, or a flattened pumpkin bread.

*I'm so screwed.*

It's only when you stop searching that you find what you're looking for, and that is precisely when I see it. A small pot of white flowers sits on a can-lined shelf. The chocolate-brown soil is dry and neglected. My hand grips the crinkling package, and I realize I've never seen this type of flower before. They have a peculiar appearance, a twisted, pointed-star pattern. Glancing down, the tag reads *Ipomoea alba* (tropical white morning-glory). *I think she'd like these, and this seems to be the only bouquet left in the store.*

I enter my car, carefully placing the flowers on the passenger seat, and realize the crisis has been averted. While these aren't the most romantic flowers in the world, I'm no longer empty-handed.

I pull up to the house where countless cars line both sides of the street. There are a *ton* of people here. As I walk toward the house holding my gift, perspiration begins to soak the creases of my button-down shirt. Loud indie music pours onto the sidewalk through the propped-open front door. I cross the threshold, seeing unknown faces chatting and smiling throughout the party. I recognize no one and no one recognizes me. *Where do I go and what should I do?* I'm all too aware that I'm the oddball with a handful of flowers who nobody is talking to. I freeze for a moment, contemplating running out the front door. *You have to find her or at least try.*

*Remember the old man withering away in his chair.*

I weave through the cliques and conversations, making my way to the deck. The glass door glides along its track, revealing additional guests outside. Yard torches frame the corners of the deck, casting an orange hue on the inhabitants. The long, skinny shadows mimic every movement of the occupants. With an awkward smile, I shuffle through the reluctant-to-move crowd.

*There she is.*

She is standing all alone on the far side of the deck, leaning her elbows on a board I constructed, looking toward the night sky. I stand as a mannequin, admiring the moment. My hand tightens around the plastic-wrapped vase of potted flowers, sending an audible *crunch* through the crisp dusk air. These vibrations swim the distance between us, entering her awaiting eardrums. Her attentive brain converts these crunchy vibrations into sound, filling her with the curiosity to discover its origin.

She spins around, revealing herself. A bright, inviting smile covers her beautiful face as she exclaims, "Oh my gosh, you came!" Witnessing her genuine excitement, all my fears are swept away by the night breeze. *But why on earth would a woman this amazing want anything to do with me?* Before I can reply, I notice her jaw is agape as she gawks toward my chest, staring at the flowers. "How did you know—? How did you know to get me *those* flowers?"

"I picked them up on the way. They're nothing special." Splotches of red-hot blood cover my features.

"Is that so? Come closer, let me see."

I stride forward and pause before her, holding the gift. She wears a dark evening dress covered with sunflower heads. The yellow fingers burst with vibrant color; the tight fabric embraces her vase-like meandering hips. She couldn't be more beautiful.

I've never thought such thoughts; I've never felt such attraction.

She extends an arm from her dress, caressing a pointed white petal. With her eyes fixated on the arrangement, she moves from one flower to the next, landing on the petals with the gentleness of a butterfly. "These are called moonflowers. I've loved these since I was a little girl. Would you like to guess why?"

As if it were a cue, when the last inflection of the question exits her mouth, the flowers open. One by one, the star patterns blossom in front of our eyes. The petals spread softly, as if by magic. I'm captivated while watching this miracle of nature unfold. The world no longer exists as before. There are no politics, no war, no famine, no tears, no measured time. Only this moment created for us to share.

When the last flower blooms, she raises her glance to meet mine.

"How did you *do* that?"

She chuckles at my childish confusion. "Moonflowers bloom every night to attract a nocturnal moth to pollinate them. When I was a girl, my grandparents planted these flowers in their yard. Every weekend, I'd beg my father to let me stay over their house. After they fell asleep, I'd climb out of my window, tip-toeing through the wet grass to watch the moonlight wake them from their slumber."

"I don't blame you, I've never witnessed anything that incredible in my life!" I say with too much excitement, my voice borderline soprano. I hand the arrangement to its new caretaker, imagining myself as a young boy seated beside her underneath the pinpricked nighttime sky. The grass dampening our backsides, the smell of rain and summer love in the air.

She extends her right hand to me. "I don't believe we ever introduced ourselves. My name is Luna."

<u>4</u>

Life has never been this great. I have everything I could ever want: a good job, a great boss, a comfortable place to live, friends, family, and most importantly, someone to share it all with. This is my lottery, and I hit it big. Working with Dusty isn't like work at all, more like an extracurricular activity with your best friend. I'll also never need a gym membership with this strenuous work, and I'm getting paid to do it! I never imagined that being alive could be so exhilarating.

Following a hard day's work building fences, decks, or sheds, I have a date with Luna to look forward to. I can't lose. Life is my own personal amusement park where one thrill leads into the next, and no matter how lame it sounds, dreams could come true. Dates with Luna are the highlight, of course. On each day's drive home, I'm eager to discover the exciting activity she planned for the evening.

Luna loves trying new things, which is great because, like most guys, I'm not much of a planner. Mostly, I think she enjoys *watching* me experience new things, and following every activity, she says, "You just expanded your bubble." She has this idea that our lives and experiences all fit inside our own personal bubble. If someone never takes risks, tries new things, or simply sticks to what they know, they will have a limited, puny bubble. "I'm *not* a small bubble person and neither are you." She commands, "I want yours to be so full, so stuffed, that one more experience will burst that engorged orb. When that happens, I want you to add one more. We're talking about your *life*. Don't you want it to be full?"

She shines brightest in these conversations, but I always make the assumption that she's only half-serious. "Each bubble-filling moment will enhance your life in some way. Once you experience something new, you'll start seeing it in places you never expected. You'll be more aware of your surroundings and gain perspective on the world we live in. You'll feel more aware, more present with each newfound memory."

This is my heaven. A life brimming with the love of the woman I adore. Since I can remember, I've been jealous of men who had this, but now I doubt that even *they* had it this great.

Our personal dates are thrilling; our mouths widen, our hands graze, and our hearts swell. But some nights we're content to drive over to my mother's house to watch some TV and sip some late-night coffee. We love those visits. Everything feels so comfortable. My mother has always been a natural at making outsiders feel like family from the moment they're introduced, and Luna was no exception. I find it hard to believe, but some days I think she cares for Luna even more than I do. This was such a relief. My mother had *never* liked any of my previous girlfriends.

"That one's not good enough for my boy," she

declared after each first meeting. This bothered me. I felt like a sheltered child, unable to make a simple decision on his own. I still dated these girls, of course, but once again, my mother *always* seemed to be right. For years, I thought I'd never find the right woman. That was until I hesitantly introduced Luna. I was petrified that my mother would repeat her bleak prophecy, until she whispered in my ear that she loved her. At that moment, I knew she'd only been protecting me all those years, and Luna was worth the wait.

I watch my mom and Luna interact as they behave like schoolgirls, giggling into their palms and playfully slapping each other on the shoulder. They talk about everything, which keeps me on edge; it usually involves something horribly embarrassing about me. Luna enjoys detailing her dream home: a house filled with forbidden possessions—soap that will never sud, unburnable candles, decorative towels, and a bed that is garnished with untouchable pillows.

Luna doesn't like to talk about it, but I know she views my mom as a mother figure. Luna never had the chance to meet her own mother; she died during labor. It's a sensitive topic only spoken of when she brings it up. It is always there though, just below the surface.

My father is a quiet man, the *strong, silent type* as my mother says. He remains passive during our visits, always present, but choosing to observe rather than participate. He has a calming presence, always prepared for a challenge, yet unwilling to let his guard down. I've known him my entire life, but I've never been able to guess what he's thinking. He would make an excellent poker player.

Luna and her father have a cordial relationship, yet a wedge remains between them. Most would expect that their mutual loss would bring them close together, but unfortunately, it created an emotional divide–an unspoken animosity stemming from the cruel trade of his daughter's life for his wife's. He never forgave her, and she could never forgive herself.

As a result, her upbringing lacked love, appreciation, and fairness. It's astonishing that she became such an incredibly optimistic and loving person.

These voids have always existed in our lives, but now we seem to have it all. Everything we desire is fulfilled in each other's companionship.

## 5

Driving home from work, my exhausted arms steer into my townhouse driveway. I don't feel up to any activities tonight; my mind and body are drained. I mosey through the door, and Luna senses that something is off. "Hi, sweetie. You sit down on the couch, and I'll come help with your boots."

I flash an appreciative glance and crawl toward the couch.

Our hallway table is covered with various fossils I've collected. I've found a few myself—small seashell imprints mostly—but I have purchased the majority. They're from the farthest reaches of the world: Argentina, Morocco, and Australia. Alien places so distant to me that they might as well be another planet. Walking past, I grab an ammonite and plop down on the scratchy fabric sofa. My sore digits trace the outlines of the multi-million-year-old specimen, feeling the imprint of this animal's body, its everlasting existence within my mortal palm. My eyes trace the spiral pattern, spinning beautifully from wide to thin. This animal died with the dinosaurs, yet here it is, in my hand. I rub my thumb against its polished smoothness and try to imagine the life it led and the incredible sights it witnessed. It is perfect. I wonder if another species will one day hold a fossil of my bones. Surely this creature never fathomed such a reality for itself.

I reach toward my laces. "Now, what did I say? My hard-working man breaks himself into a thousand pieces every day, and when he comes home, I put the puzzle back together." She bends down on one knee and unravels my tan, frayed laces.

I sink into the couch and can't help but admire those warm, comforting green eyes. She tugs each steel-toed boot off my beaten-down feet, and the rush of fresh blood careens into my heels like a burst levee. The waters continue to rise, the blood surging and swelling my phalanges. Without a word, Luna begins massaging both feet. Her tender touch forces the flood waters to recede back into the sea.

"My feet are *killing* me, Tick." The whimper trails off my pouting lips.

"Gosh, you are such a pansy. But you're *my* pansy. Why don't you take a little nap while I finish cooking dinner?" she whispers. Her lotion smells of warm, summertime lavender.

Slouched with my head jammed between the pillows and wearing my dirty, wood-shaving covered clothes, I'd never been so comfortable. "That sounds like a good idea. Just for a minute."

My eyes close and I'm instantly swept away.

A delicious aroma awakens me. A steaming plate filled with crusted chicken and thick, buttery noodles is seated before me.

Luna sits on the couch and hands me a glass of creamy white milk. "Let's eat, baby. It'll make you feel better." When she looks at me, I get that feeling like when a shooting star falls precisely in my eye line, as if it fell just for me. *She loves me. This is love.* While staring at her flawless face, I think that this *must* be a fantasy.

Luna nods her head toward my plate and we begin eating. She switches on my favorite TV show and covers her lap with a blanket I gave her on our six-month anniversary. While shopping one day, we stumbled across the blanket. She couldn't stop rubbing it against her cheek in the aisle, repeating that it was the *coziest* thing she'd ever felt. I returned the following day to buy it. I'd never think such a thing would be a big deal, but when she unwrapped the present, she made me feel like a hero. She moved in shortly after, and it's been by her side ever since.

During dinner, chuckles release through our nostrils as my taste buds scream with ecstasy. Her full-mouthed smile causes her dimples to be more pronounced, her soul more radiant. This is the greatest meal I've ever eaten.

We've been dating for nine months, but each day, my heart grows fonder. Nobody besides my mother has cared for me like this, and I'm not certain I'll ever grow accustomed to it. Do rich people remember being poor? Or does their former life wind up feeling like someone else's bad dream?

When the credits roll and our plates are empty, Luna

fidgets with the countless bobby pins in her chocolate hair. "Kind of worked out with you being tired. I didn't plan anything to do tonight." Her front teeth clamp down on a bundle of pins.

My jaw drops onto my clean plate. "Let's get you to the emergency room. Are you okay?"

She punches my sore arm, her lips in a playful grimace. "Hey, everybody needs a day off. But since you're *so* disappointed, you can take me for a walk in Old Town."

"After that incredible dinner, I'm your slave."

Old Town is a historic part of the city that's near our home. While the city has modernized, the aptly named Old Town still has the original cobblestone roads. Unique shops, quirky restaurants, and dimly lit pubs line the streets. There is never a shortage of people-watching potential on the walking mall, but I know the real reason she loves it there–the dogs. No mutt is safe when the Luna-tick latches onto the unsuspecting canines, showering their scruffy heads with hundreds of unsolicited stranger kisses.

I throw on some clean clothes, and we head down the street, holding hands. Along the path, we walk past an old cemetery. Luna turns to me and says, "It's odd to think those buried people were the former residents of this place. Their sweat and blood built these buildings, their feet walked this street, their hands held the ones they loved." She flexes her grip. "I used to think of old people as always being *old*, or dead people as always being *dead*. But, obviously, that's wrong. Underneath those carved stones are people, all with their own lives, their own problems, their own happiness, and their own families. Hard-working people, venturing home to recharge, repeating this process each day until they found themselves here.

"As I've grown older, I've realized that whenever and wherever we walk, each step is leading toward that lonely hole in the earth. Every person in this world, from the richest executive to the poorest beggar, all share the same boring, gloomy destiny. From that moment, I promised myself to make every moment *before* that day the best I could." She pauses. "Sorry, I didn't intend to get all *heavy*, but I know I can be a little much sometimes and wanted you to understand. Arden, we are connected. I knew it from the moment we met. I want the best for you, because a happy *you* makes a happy *me*. Does that make any sense?"

We've passed multiple dogs that Luna hasn't batted an eye at, so I know she's serious. "Of course it makes sense. We've only been together for a short time, but *you* make me happy," I reply, digging my hands inside my jean pockets.

"But is that enough? Will *I* be enough in a few years? You make me happy, too, and although it hasn't been long, we should talk about the future."

*Whoa.* Although I'm crazy about this woman, the abruptness catches me off guard.

"Okay, no time like the present."

We sit on a wooden bench, our gazes directed toward a coming sunset. "Okay, I'll jump right in. I know you enjoy working for Dusty, and you know I love Dusty, too. You've been working there for a year and have become great at your job. It's rare to work for somebody who you're good friends with, and I'm glad you have that. My question is: do you love the *job* or do you simply enjoy being around Dusty?"

I try to conceal my defensiveness. "I mean, this is a little odd considering we've never talked about this. Yes, the job is tough and frustrating at times, but what job isn't? Where is this coming from?"

Luna raises her hands and leans back. "Okay, okay. I'm not trying to start an argument. I'm just trying to have a discussion with you. I'd never diminish your accomplishments; you've done well for yourself. I'm only curious about your ambitions and where you'd like to be someday. If you see yourself in carpentry, then that's fine! But I hope you know there's more to life than working to pay the bills. To be truly happy, we need to be fulfilled in every area of our lives, and I can't give that all to you. So, answer me this, and I'll stop: on the drive home after work, are you fulfilled?"

My eyebrows bunch together. "Well, no. But I've never had that with *any* job. I doubt it even exists."

"I disagree. I thought the same way until I became a teacher. I'd slaved at countless professions: restaurants, administrative, healthcare, and customer service. None seemed to fit, and the more I tried to squeeze myself into the box, the worse it felt. It's not that these jobs were horrible; they each had their own redeeming qualities. Despite this, no matter how hard I tried to convince myself otherwise, none gave me fulfillment. The truth is, I didn't want to be convinced. My worst fear has always been to settle; my soul craved the inner peace. That's when I decided to make the change. Careers are like relationships, you know. Everyone suffers through crap before finding the *one*. This is normal. Nobody finds their dream occupation right off the bat. I hope you know it's not too late to make a change, to become the person you're meant to be and surpass the potential that everyone sees in you."

The sun dips behind the wavy mountain range, projecting an orange warmth upon the purple cloud-splattered sky. The dazzling sunsets here in Tennessee could inspire even the most lackluster artist. I grab a nearby stone and rub my thumb along its smooth edge. These types of conversations seem to suffocate me, bringing on that old familiar feeling. My heart fluttering within my throat, my forehead tingles with creeping anxiety as the world weighs on my shoulders. Its unforgiving mouth leans into my ear, the vacant face whispering that I'm the architect of my own future. The responsibility is too much to bear. I could never decide on anything, so I decided on nothing.

I finally reply, "Sorry for getting all worked up. As always, you're right. I wish I could commit, really. I just worry that whatever decision I make will be wrong, and I'll wind up miserable, forced to start over again."

I glance her way; the sight of her always catches me off guard. Her beauty is enough to stop the sunset in its tracks.

"Once again, *normal*. In my experience, doing something you're interested in makes for a successful career. Believe it or not, Ard, but I know you. I can feel when you're unhappy, even in the slightest. You and I are just on the same wavelength. So, what interests you?"

"Could I get paid to stare at you?" The smooth rock twists and turns inside my grip. "I'm *great* at being wrong; I could be a meteorologist."

Luna stares at my palm with curiosity painted across her face. Her mahogany hair shines as she says, "I think the answer is in your hands."

I look down at my opened grip. The pebble winks in the dying light. "You don't mean an archaeologist. No way, not me. I mean, that was my childhood dream, but that's crazy."

"Why is it crazy to do something you love? Something you've wanted your entire life but somehow convinced yourself you aren't good enough for? Wouldn't you like to prove yourself wrong?"

*I would.* "That's too much schooling. There's no way I could handle it."

"Not with that attitude. You're smart, much brighter than you realize."

I blush, shaking my head. "Even if I went for something like that, I'd have to travel and move."

"That's fine, my job is mobile. You can't get rid of me that easy," she says with a flutter of her eyelashes.

The more I think about this, the more excited I become. It's one of those moments where something inside of you *clicks*, a key's teeth fitting perfectly in a lock cylinder. Luna witnesses this new energy enter my soul, and she beams with pride. "It wouldn't hurt to start taking some classes. You really think this is a good idea?"

Her lips spread as her head nods.

"The idea's always been in the back of my mind, but I've brushed it off. It *does* make sense."

The stars peek out from their hiding places as the streetlights flicker on, illuminating the path to our new world.

"Let's get you home, Mr. Fossil. We've got some digging to do."

"I can't wait to tell Dusty."

<u>6</u>

Luna and I spend the evening researching various schools' programs–our wide eyes glued to the computer screen, our favorite coffee mugs twirling with steam, each foot in its favorite slipper. Despite the excitement, we finally decide it's time for sleep.

Something strange happens the following morning: I rise *before* my alarm. In addition, I don't feel the urge to beeline toward my coffee maker. Still, I have a cup, just to ward off the caffeine shakes. While sipping my day-starter, I think this must be what it's like to wake up with a sense of purpose. I could grow accustomed to this. I feel excited, clear, and alive. Time seems to be working *for* me instead of against me.

I stare out the living room window, watching the world transform from black-and-white to color. A sudden realization occurs that it's time to move forward in *every* way. I've waited long enough to make the biggest decision of my life.

I keep quiet in the mornings to not wake Luna, knowing she needs the extra hour of sleep to be attentive for the children. I creep into the bedroom with a glass of cold water, its clinking ice cubes causing her to stir underneath the disheveled covers. "Good morning, my love," I whisper as the foggy glass finds its place on the nightstand, its sweat beads gathering around the base. I gently sit on the bed's edge. "I can't stay, have to run, but I wanted to say I had a wonderful time last night." She smiles, nodding with closed eyes while bunching her favorite blanket beneath her creased cheek. I kiss her forehead lightly. "Oh, and one more little thing. Will you marry me?"

Her eyes burst open in disbelief, dilating when her glance lands on the diamond and sapphire encrusted ring. She props up on her elbows, and her mouth falls to the mattress.

"What took you so long?" she asks as I slide the ring on her dainty finger. It locks in place perfectly.

"I bought this ring a month after we met. I never doubted that you're the woman I want to spend the rest of my life with. I want to care for you. I want to be there when you cry. I want to be there when you smile. Forever, Tick."

Her arms swaddle my body, and I breathe her sweet scent into my lungs, smiling and shedding a tear against her neckline. Her left hand peels from my shoulder as she gazes into the jewel.

" *Wow.* Am I dreaming? I must be asleep, so please don't wake me."

We pull away, our hands refusing to separate, still cupped around each other's elbows.

"I'll take that as a... *yes.*"

She nods breathlessly, swallowing hard and then letting out a hearty laugh. Her palm covers her mouth as her left hand raises to her eye line. The blue sapphires return her stare, reflected in her iris, flashing them teal. An instant bond is forged.

"I had a more thought-out engagement plan, but I couldn't wait any longer. I love you," I say into her eyes, declaring it with more passion than ever in my life.

"It's perfect. It's all perfect. I love you, too."

"Go back to sleep, if you can, and we'll talk tonight. We have lots to discuss, but now isn't the time, Ms. Morning Breath."

We part ways with matching smiles, so wide that every tooth is exposed.

My morning drive is revitalized as I swap the radio's dull music for roadside silence. To my surprise, the silence *lacks* stillness as my mind races with promising ideas and sounds of the waking world. Despite being a chilly dawn, my windows are down, tucked into the doorframes. The crisp air nibbles my skin and cleanses my soul.

The faraway call of migratory birds echo above, positioned in their famous "V" formation. My inquisitive mind wonders how they coordinate such a dramatic feat. It must be superb communication skills and a willingness to cooperate for the group's well-being—skills that become more scarce with each human generation. The birds seek only survival, understanding that the best way to accomplish that is to trust one another. The *real world*—where the strongest survive but still not without the help of others.

Their wings graze a moon that works overtime, it hangs as a five-cent piece in the morning sky, face and all.

How many moments like this have I missed? How often have I been wrapped up in my trivial life that I ignored the surrounding miracles above my head? Tangled in the spindly web of my minuscule problems, fears, and insecurities. Unable to see clearly, confined to shallow breaths. Have I ever been content to be entirely passive, an unbiased observer of this reality? A witness to its wonder, acknowledging that all my kicking and screaming against its ancient wheel of time is futile—to finally go with the flow instead of against the grain. Of all the power in this world, the greatest strength of all is to submit to its will. Fate, destiny, whatever you want to call it. But, maybe those carved routes can only take one so far. Perhaps they can only present a person with options, a crossroads where a choice must be made. Fate cannot make the horse drink the water. That's where I currently stand, at a fork in the road. I've finally decided on a route.

*She said yes. I cannot believe I'm engaged to the woman of my dreams.*

My car idles beneath a red stop light beside the shop's parking lot, and I see a strange sight. I'm the first one here. Every day I arrive a half hour prior to the other workers, but Dusty *always* beats me here. He arrives early to unlock the doors, map out the day's work orders, and manage the bookkeeping. He never allows anyone but himself to handle these daily tasks, always insisting on executing them himself. "Heavy is the crown, Ard," he says each time I suggest hiring additional help.

He is *never* late—well, except for that one morning he slept in. The guys and I decided not to call him, and he finally arrived at 9 a.m., embarrassed and disheveled. Riddled with misaligned buttons and greasy hair mashed down on the left side of his head but sticking straight up on the right. He stammered through a nonsensical daylight savings explanation even though it was summer, as if he had to answer to *us.* It was all pretty comical to watch; the guys never let him live that one down.

The light turns green, and I switch off my blinker. *I'll swing by his place and save him the trouble. It's just down the road. I can even surprise him with the good news!*

My tires turn into the driveway, stopping behind Dusty's tan work truck, and my suspicions are confirmed. "Poor guy must be sleeping like a baby, but he's in for a rude awakening!" The appearance of Dusty's house wouldn't give the impression that a professional carpenter lives here. His one-level rancher's walkway carves a wooded path to the porch. It's littered with sun-bleached, warped, and missing boards. The house is also in rough shape. Misshapen and torn shingles are scattered throughout the front yard like picked scabs, the patchy roof showing the open wounds of their departure.

I hopscotch across the walkway, contemplating how to ask if he needs help to fix the place up. Now that I think about it, he *has* mentioned it before. But after a long day on the job, the last thing I wanted to think about was *more* woodworking. *I've been making excuses to not help my friend. I'd want someone's help if I were him.*

My hand reaches for the black handle of the screen door, noticing it's peppered with dry, flaky sections of paint, its undercoat being slowly exposed with each grasp. Funny enough, the base color is *more* appealing than the finished black outer coat. This simple doorknob is putting on an act, attempting to be something it is not. Each person's touch brings it closer to realizing its true potential, to restoring its natural beauty. Although not reflective, I see myself in this doorknob—the *new* me. I refuse to be masked by the world or at the mercy of the wind. I rub my abrasive palm against its surface, knocking off a few more chips, one step closer. I snicker at the pure insanity of this moment.

My knuckles rap on Dusty's front door, and the countdown to *freak-out* commences. My flattened backside presses against the squeaking storm door as I wait, but there is no answer. I knock again. Nothing but silence is returned.

The door's coiled spring compresses and moans.

*Hmmm, that's strange.* I cup my eyes against the inlaid window, peeking inside the living room. *He's not in there.* "Dusty! Hey man, think you slept in again. Let's get a move on, the boss is a real hard-ass!"

A dog barks. I turn to see a woman jogging along the road with her pet. A turquoise and pink wisp sunrise fills the empty space in their portrait. I smile and offer a wave as she returns the gesture.

Another uneventful minute passes, and I realize he isn't waking up. I try calling his phone but it diverts to voicemail. *I don't want to pound on the door like the police.* I twist the doorknob, and it pops open easily. I step through the threshold, calling out once again, "Dusty, it's me. Please don't call the cops. You've slept in. It's time to go to work."

The house is stagnant, hushed.

Not long ago, this home would've been bursting with energy: Dusty's two boys running wild, their mother in hot pursuit, attempting to dress them for school, herding them out the door with full lunch pails, reminding them to zip up their jackets. But following their ruthless divorce, Dusty's former spouse received full custody and moved to the west coast. At least that's what he's told me. It's hard to imagine Dusty in that life and role; this one is all I've known. *I should ask more about his family. I wonder if they're still close.*

My heavy boots stamp the living room carpet, marking their path toward the hallway. I've been underneath this roof countless times, but before now, I've never noticed how impersonal his house appears. There are no family pictures on the cream walls, only a handful of landscape paintings. If I didn't know any better, I'd assume this was a rental and the nitpicking landlord didn't allow any personalization. The reality is that Dusty has owned this house for over ten years.

My steps locate Dusty's closed bedroom door. *Maybe that's why he couldn't hear me.* My fingertips tap against the wood. "Hey, it's Ard. Don't make me walk in on something that'll make me bleach my eyes!"

Still, no response.

*He might've taken some sleeping medicine; maybe he's sick.* "Quit shaving your legs, I'm coming in!" I twist the golden knob and swing the white, wooden door open. As its inward rotation reveals the inner room, the walls look *dirty—*

*MOWWRWW!*

A screeching, blurry ball of sound dashes between my legs and into the hallway behind me. I turn, seeing a flash of black and tail and realize it was Dusty's cat.

With my heart thumping, I turn back toward the room. "Damn, Dusty, why are cats so—"

Someone is slumped over in his bed. The top half of their skull is gone. Mangled chunks and wet strings of meat dangle atop a bottom row of broken, gore-covered teeth. My brain struggles to interpret what my eyes are seeing. *A man?* His bleached arms are hugged loosely around the long barrel of a flat-black shotgun, the weapon wedged against his torso. A kickstand. The bed is a standing pool of blood. In those red waters, a set of pale, bare feet stand walleyed, half submersed at the bottom of the bed.

The surrounding walls *are* dirty, but the ceiling is worse.

My stomach fills with lead—I've never witnessed such a sight. The splattered bedroom resembles horror film scenes, only *much* worse. Its heinous details are well beyond any director's twisted imagination—as it should be. It should not exist on this earth. A chunky, molasses glob breaks off the man's jagged front tooth, splashing into the ever-expanding swamp. I'm uncertain whether to vomit or cry. Millions of frantic thoughts sprint through my mind. *Did someone do this to him? Everybody loves Dusty, right? There's no way he did this to himself. He would never.*

*Right?*

Now I'm crying, weeping like never before. The tears dissimilar to the teenage fallout of fighting with my parents—scurrying up the carpeted stairs, the door slamming, burying my head inside the yellowed pillowcase. The hormone-enriched beads of water painting a blotchy, abstract self-portrait for no one to admire. Nothing in comparison to when I first moved out on my own; when the real world didn't sugarcoat its lack of respect for my ambitions or plans. With streaked cheeks, I'd punch a pathetic, fist-sized hole in the apartment's drywall, submitting to the pent-up emotions of failure, the rivulets maturing to rivers during my adult tantrum.

I'm crying harder than I ever dreamed possible. Screaming, careless of who will hear, see, or think of me. These are my first true tears, and I wish I would've died ignorant. Every agonizing emotion I'm capable of overflows, seeping out of the five million pores of my trembling body.

Anxiety drips through my fingertips, guilt fills the soles of my shoes, anger creases the corners of my mouth, shame travels along my notched spine, and sadness encompasses everything I am.

*There's something on the nightstand.*

A folded paper, sprayed with distorted, cherry spots. I grab the note, unconcerned with what the detective might say about tainting evidence. The paper unfolds and crinkles in my abrupt grip, unveiling bold letters.

**Tell the kids I love them.**

**Tell the kids I'm sorry.**

It's Dusty's handwriting, and the world is crumbling before my eyes.

My nerves have been stunned. The deadened sensation originates at my fingertips, slithering against gravity into my palms, forearms, all the way to my ears. A phantom anesthetic in my veins.

The gut-wrenching note releases from my grasp as if it were on fire, parachuting to the stained carpet as I run toward the entrance of the house. This was my best friend in the entire world, yet this is the last place I want to be.

Please, get me away from seeing his insides spread across the room like an amateur's attempt at conceptual art. Please, take me away from the awful last words he penned, far from the stench of bodily waste and decay that may never depart my nostrils.

While stumbling down the hall, the lonely landscape painting hangs in the corridor. My palms rub against my mannequin cheeks, clearing the blurred vision through my webbed eyelashes.

The portrait depicts a teal, rushing river surrounded by fluffy green trees. The gushing waves send playful sprays of white against big, brown, rounded boulders. Their rough stone bodies slowly shaped and formed by a thousand years of erosive water. Mother Nature: the world's slowest, most painstakingly perfectionist sculptor. A giant, snow-capped mountain stands watch in the background where not a single cloud lingers in the clear, baby blue sky. Here is a place where nothing could ever go wrong, a setting where every dream comes true, and each day is as peaceful as a monk's soul.

*What a lie. What a blatant fucking lie.*

I grasp each side of its decorative gold frame and send the abomination flying through the static air of the living room. The surprisingly aerodynamic frame soars with the grace of an elementary school paper airplane until its inevitable crash landing. The repulsive scenery smashes through Dusty's coffee table, huge glass shards and colorful dried paint globs bursting from the impact. The shattered fantasy world is suddenly more realistic.

A lust for blood and destruction causes my brain to float inside its skull. I'll go room to room and splinter every mirror, smash every dish, kick a hole in every wall, and saw every bit of furniture in half. When there's nothing left to destroy, I'll burn it down. I'll torch this whole forsaken hellhole to the ground. That would be better than anyone else witnessing what happened inside that room.

I hate this house, but I don't want to stay inside for another second, even if it was to destroy it. My numbed hand throws the flimsy screen door open as the same woman and dog are returning from their tranquil walk. The door crashes into the house's vinyl siding with a reverberating BANG as the woman directs her startled attention toward me. Her fearful, ghastly expression mirrors my own as she realizes that I'm either coming to kill her or something is terribly wrong.

The pair remain stationary, cautious.

I move in their direction, tripping over my own limbs, trying to explain as cold tears flow in the new-day sun. The dog's leash pulls taut as a growl rumbles against its frayed collar. "I need you to call the police—an ambulance. Anyone that can help! My friend is dead."

I'm deaf to my own voice as my rubber feet travel the wooden walkway.

"He's *dead!*" My foot fails to find the needed support on the next step, and my knee crashes against the boards–my foot wedged where a board should be. My body slumps, elbows on the splintered walkway, and my forehead leans against the warm boards.

The world goes silent as I remain crippled, paralyzed inside my own mind. The entire planet continues spinning on its invisible axis, while I'm suspended in time.

The paramedics begin to arrive. The swollen trucks are all equipped with flashing lights, blaring horns. Little do they know, there is no emergency. A frenzy of movement erupts as the vehicles give birth to their heroic passengers who commence preparation for life-saving attempts. A uniformed scout is sent into the dark house to assess the situation. I watch as he disappears into the mouth of the beast.

In what could have been thirty minutes or thirty seconds, he exits the home, giving a faint shake of his head to the awaiting crew. The movement grinds to a halt as the workers realize there is no rush.

The strangest thing about this whole scene was the scout's expression when he exited the home—he had *none*. What he found inside must've caused him zero panic. *Nothing unusual here, boys. Just another headless man.* How many scenes such as this, how many dead people did it take to become that numb? Ten, fifty, a hundred?

Dozens of neighbors creep out of their comfortable homes, all standing on their sidewalks to get a glimpse of the action. Some hold briefcases, others cradle coffee mugs, all of their inquisitive heads on a swivel.

A big damn show.

Despite the numerous people watching the spectacle, no one has approached the house or the emergency workers to retrieve any information.

*Did they know Dusty, or are they looking for some gossip? Now that I think about it, Dusty never mentioned being close to his neighbors—or anyone, for that matter.*

"—did you hear me, son?" A policeman is standing beside me.

"No."

"Okay, I need to ask you a few questions. Is that all right?" The cop proceeds with his line of questioning, asking if I pulled the trigger, but in a trained, professional way. I sense that every move he makes is *by the book*, even though I've never read it. I can only stare at his badge, tracing its reinforced, pointed edges, the subdued engraving on its sunflower face, and contemplating the bottomless weight it carries.

As I'm answering with my hazy, third person recollection, a gurney is wheeled out of the house. Glazed eyes look past the policeman as my wooden mouth communicates. Three men transport a heavy, stuffed black bag across the bumpy yard, its contents subtly shifting with each wheel's rotation on the rutted crabgrass. As much as they try to remain quiet, this is a noisy affair. The metal joints creak against the bag's internal weight, the purple shocks whine, and the green cushion exhales a hearty mouthful with each bump. The heavy black zipper is trusted to hold tight, teeth biting into teeth, shielding the outside world from its abhorrent filler–my best friend.

Maybe the crowd has gone silent; maybe the state has been gagged. Just like when a city loses power for an evening, its sheltered citizens stunned and afraid of the visible stars above them. A top-hatted magician snapping the veil away, exposing the breath-stealing sight. They can see the entire pixelated galaxy above their craned heads, a giant gash torn in the fabric of our universe.

Its expanse and timelessness drops an anchor into their stomachs and wraps a charley horse around their hearts.

The overworking brains behind their globed eyeballs fear an extraterrestrial event. The emergency lines overflow with frantic voices. But it has always been there; a collection of matter as old as time itself, almost within arm's reach, but masked by a million porch lights.

Their world is briefly without light pollution; mine is without noise. I'm able to soak up every scrap of this sound. The million sounds of a loaded gurney. And I'll side with the city dwellers–it is unsettling, abnormal, and petrifying.

The trio of men transporting the corpse are equipped with the same emotionless expression as the scout: not happy, not sad, but human statues. Their minds wondering what time they'll go home tonight, how they'll spend their day off, or why the brain always seems to fall directly in the deceased person's lap. While staring at the workers, I realize that I, too, am without expression.

Maybe all it takes is one, after all.

## 7

Static white noise lingers in the background. Luna is speaking, but I can't seem to concentrate. Perhaps I don't want to. Her muffled voice attempts to pierce my boxed ears. "Honey, please listen for a moment. I know you've had a hard time dealing with this situation, but maybe we can find a new job for you today."

A lingering distaste sticks against the roof of my mouth. "I'm not in the mood. To be honest, that is the absolute *last* thing I'd like to do today."

"Well, when might you be ready, sweetheart? I mean, the funeral was over two months ago. I think Dusty would want you to move on."

"Are you serious? *Move on?* The only thing Dusty wanted was to be headless—like you even understand."

"I do understand," she says. "I understand that this was *not* your fault."

"Oh, I know *that*," I snap at the woman I once adored, coiling tight against my scales.

After a long pause, she replies, "What are you saying, that it's *my* fault?"

"Well, if you didn't have me running around the entire world every day, doing your stupid bubble bullshit, then I would've noticed that something was wrong." My fangs are exposed.

"I don't know how to respond to that–"

"Oh, sure you do, Miss Fucking-Know-It-All. Luna's got all the answers. 'Oh, just do this, just do that. Drop everything and go to college! Arden, go out and find another meaningless job; time to get over your dead best friend.' You put on a front that you have it all together, but you don't know shit. All you are is a teacher in a dumpy local school who's engaged to a piece of trash like me." I'm standing, uncoiled as the venom spews from my needled teeth.

I wait for a reply. *Yeah, say something. Go ahead, bitch. It's all your fault. Everything.*

"Did you mean *any* of that?" she replies, her throat squeezing the vocal cords.

The venom has soured my thoughts. "Every. Damn. Word."

A single tear plunges from those big, forest green supernovas I fell in love with so long ago. She blinks the emotion away and softly nods her head. The teardrop breaks off her jawline, falling to the floor like the first sign of a torrential downpour. Before it impacts the carpet, she silently moves toward the front door. She gathers her purse, grasps her jingling keys, and opens the door to our once happy home. Stepping through the entryway into the blinding light, she pulls the door shut without looking back. The latch engages, and I'm reassured she is gone, comforted that I can shut myself off again.

*She'll be back, anyways. She always comes back. How many times have we fought like this? It seems almost daily, but I can't keep track anymore. Whatever, doesn't matter, she'll be back.*

I sit on the couch, letting the anger regress into my subconscious. She'd never leave me, and even if she did, she'd come to get her belongings. If she comes with her empty cardboard boxes, I'll apologize, and we'll make up like always. I know she'd at least return for her favorite blanket.

*Wait, her blanket isn't in its usual place on the rocking chair by the fireplace, but maybe it's in the bedroom.* Making my way to the back room, it's not there either. I search the entire house, including the washing machine, and it's nowhere to be found.

In addition to the blanket, the house does seem rather empty. I return to our bedroom, throwing the closet door open. What I find leaves me stunned. Where there was once a sprawling selection of women's attire, all arranged according to color, there is now vacant space.

*This can't be. How could this happen?* She didn't leave today with anything but her purse. *It couldn't be possible that I didn't notice her moving out, box by box.*

Moving to our shared dresser, I open drawer after drawer.

Nothing.

Nothing.

Nothing—

A ring stares back at me. A diamond ring adorned with bright blue sapphire stones. The ring I gave to her. It stands all alone against the particle board. Its unexpected presence rips the organs from my chest.

I slam the drawer shut with every scrap of force I can muster. Then I yank it back open and slam it again. And then again. I slam the drawer back and forth like a hungry saw through fresh wood, pulling it wide open until it hits the stopping point and then sending it speeding into the wooden furniture with a **CRASH**. I hear the ring pinballing against the wood, making tiny pockmarks as it whips about like a car crash victim without a seatbelt.

The TV atop the dresser wobbles wildly, out of rhythm with the violent motion. With my left palm planted on the dresser, my right hand grasps the drawer pull and uppercut punches the sliding drawer closed. My thin-skinned knuckles collide into the hard, ornate backing and the television gives up its balancing act, smashing onto the hardwood floor. "Shit! You've got to be kidding me!"

I begin pacing around the house, talking to no one. "You bitch—FUCKING BITCH!" My fingers dial her number. The ringer chimes twice and diverts to voicemail. *She ignored my call.* "Fine, I don't want to talk to you either!" My phone sails across the living room and tumbles underneath the sofa.

My brain swells with the notion of a drink. A nice, stiff drink is just what my watering mouth craves. Ripping the freezer door open, a bottle of southern whiskey is buried beneath a mountain of frozen peas. I hate the taste of liquor, but something tells me, *Not today, you don't.*

Grabbing a coffee mug off the counter, I start to pour. The amber liquid splashes into the cup as the air bubbles float like balloons inside the thick, clear bottle. Glug, glug, glug. The ceramic mug touches my lips as that familiar, pungent, unforgiving scent scorches my nostrils.

I open my throat *porno* wide to let it slide right down. It does, and although that bottle has been in the freezer for months, the sensation it injects is pure, heavenly summertime warmth. The magic fluid travels down my esophagus as a mini-ball of blue flame. The liquor careens into my abdomen, coating and tracing the entire organ. I can *see* the physical shape of my own concealed stomach through the outlining sensations.

*That is exactly what I needed—a little something to take the edge off.* Standing at the counter with one hand on the glass and the other on the bottle, I can't help but think, *That was much better than I expected. Who wouldn't want to chase that feeling every day?* Alcoholism suddenly makes perfect sense to me.

The gooseflesh transforms my skin into braille. I wonder what it says.

My head becomes the bubbles within the bottle, threatening to float against the popcorned ceiling if it wasn't attached to my shoulders. I feel carefree and better than I have in a long time. I think I'll have another.

Raising the glass, I'm reminded of how the young me would pinch his nose and eyes closed to muscle down a stiff drink. I chuckle at the absurdity of my past self and introduce the liquor into my digestive system without a wince. *Even better than the first.* The hard liquid floods my mind, triggering my raw thoughts to spew into the world.

"Why would he leave me with sole power of attorney? *Me?* Didn't he have somebody—*anybody*—else that could deal with his shit? I mean, his kids aren't even teenagers, and I'm *assuming* he didn't trust his ex-wife, but *damn!* Who does that to their best friend? If he only knew. Go ahead, Mr. Hot Shot Lawyer, sell the business, cash out the life insurance, sell his house—not that anyone would ever want to move in. No, I don't feel bad for dumping all his belongings because his kids got the money. That's the least anyone could do for them, considering they're going to be traumatized for the rest of their lives. How could anyone do that to their kids?"

Glug, glug, glug.

"He left me in charge, though. Yeah, he must've thought the world of me; I'm so flattered. Well, I wonder if his opinion would change if he knew what *I* thought of *him*. I hate you, son of a bitch. I hope those religious people are right and you *are* burning in hell. Mortal sin, huh? Killing yourself is a one-way, all-expense paid ticket to the pit.

"Some devout followers pick and choose when to apply and when to ignore this belief when their own loved one eats a bullet sandwich. But in your case, I hope it's true, because you left *us* in hell. Your poor kids will spend their lives wondering why they weren't enough for Daddy to tough out whatever bullshit was going on in his life, having to explain to every person that, 'No, you can't meet my dad. His head blew away like a dandelion.'

"Selfish prick. You take yourself out and we're left here to pick up your skull pieces, wondering what *we* did wrong. How about your funeral? Closed casket, as you can imagine. The mother of your children sobbed as she blamed herself, wondering aloud about who will teach the boys how to play sports or how to be a man. Not you. Each person silent, struggling to find something good to say. Anything to steer away from the headless elephant in the room. Your family reciting rehearsed speeches about better times, fond memories of your life. Bittersweet smiles. Disingenuous and forced laughter. Every person wondering, 'Why couldn't he slit his wrists or swallow some painkillers like a normal person?' That's because Dusty's motto was, 'Be the best at whatever you do, and do it right the first time.' You sure did. This wasn't a cry for help. This wasn't a trial run."

Glug, glug, glug.

I think of the abandoned ring inside the dresser drawer–once a symbol of commitment, hope, and love. Another casualty attributed to Dusty.

*Everyone is suffering the aftershocks of your earthquake.*

*I don't remember falling asleep,* my groggy mind thinks as I find myself lying on the kitchen floor. The world seems ablaze as a remote, flame-engulfed star scorches my retinas. Its invisible, yet powerful beams saturate my skin. Rays of light that traveled seven minutes to reach this planet, finding their way through my window, only to land on my hungover self. *What a crappy fate.*

I squint at the new day sun as it slowly burns the darkness from the sky.

My mouth tastes horrible as I lift myself to one elbow on the crumby floor. As I stand, the Earth attempts to put me right back down. My hands grip the kitchen counter. I could be trapped inside a lava lamp.

*I'm out of booze. Well, maybe that's a blessing in disguise because I feel like trash that was run over by the garbage truck.* A slight scent of spilled liquor finds its way into my unsuspecting nostrils. *My mouth is watering again—and not in a good way.* I wobble over to the kitchen sink with bulging, cartoon character cheeks, and piping hot magma pours from my mouth into the basin. Chunky mats of sludge splash and stick to the round basin, some finding its way onto the drywall. I dry heave at the sight and stench, appalled that this grotesque mesh was inside of me. My breathless, tear-streaked face is laced with thick, swollen veins creating roadmaps along my crimson forehead and neck.

*It's over.* I catch my breath while rinsing out the sink, already feeling much better. "Had to get that demon out!" I chug a hefty serving of tap water straight from the faucet, savoring its metallic, fluoride-enhanced flavor.

*I should get out of the house for a bit. Some fresh air might be good. Get my mind off things.*

Brushing my teeth feels better than the first shower after a weekend camping trip, reborn and breathing ice. I leave the house carrying only my wallet, abandoning my phone. The device is still lying underneath the living room furniture, the battery withering away. Maybe calls are stacking up, possibly important ones, but who cares? Not me. I have nobody to talk to.

Walking into Old Town with an empty front pocket, I feel exhilarated, unplugged, detached from any stress, separated from everyone. Even though the shopping strip is lined with colorful, enticing stores, I enter only one. At the far end of the walking mall is a sign reading one word: *Spirits.*

## 8

I've lost track of the days, but this routine has become my new religion—a reason to wake up in the morning (or afternoon). Every new lifestyle has its adjustment period, though. I learned the hard way to select a different type of liquor each day, as the smell of the previous night's drink is unbearable the following day.

Wake up, throw up, drink, repeat.

I don't care if time is slow or flying by. I'm not paying attention anymore. Escaping my thoughts is the goal, but alcohol only serves to amplify them—at least while I'm awake. What I'm really after is sleep. After much incoherent experimentation, I've learned how to position myself to avoid the spins, allowing me to sleep like a baby—a thoughtless, stress-free, anywhere-is-comfortable type of sleep. Perfect, dreamless rest so deep that you get a taste of non-existence, never returning from the void and not knowing the difference.

*What reason do I have to be conscious anyway?*

I never pictured I'd wind up alone, but each day is more miserable than the last. I've come to the conclusion that this *is* my life. Sure, there must be someone out there who is more depressed than I am—and for better reasons—but that doesn't ease my suffering. On the contrary, it strengthens my resolve. I couldn't *imagine* being worse off. Even though it's possible, I can't fathom the possibility of sinking deeper.

My self-confidence is beneath the soil while my self-consciousness is above the clouds.

I feel more emotionally battered than a low-end psychiatrist, selflessly soaking up every patient's problems, issues, and insecurities. A dirty emotional punching bag caked with more layers of filth than a polygraph examiner following a fourteen-hour shift. All the polluted secrets, held shut for decades, now exposed to the air you breathe. The weight off their shoulders is transferred to your own.

These thoughts consume me, breeding in the darkest reaches of my mind where vileness rears its ugly offspring.

Depression feels as though the entire world is focused on your life while simultaneously ignoring you. A negative form of attention. Paparazzi without the status. All those flashing cameras and smiling faces desperate to capture your every move, just to mock your existence.

Despite my endless efforts, I cannot snap out of this downward spiral. Life cannot be *that* bad, right? Yet, I cannot shake the sensation that an invisible anchor is tied to my feet—pulling, dragging as I sink further and deeper below the silent ripples of a bottomless, unforgiving ocean.

As my tired arms thrash and my decreasing air bubbles float toward the surface, I greet the depths.

## 9

I'm taking a day off drinking. I need it. My brain is in a constant state of fog, dehydrated and clouded by the liquor.

I spend the afternoon pacing around my home, painfully sober, and mentally thanking my parents for paying six months advance rent to help me take some time off. I visit rooms that have been abandoned for weeks, smelling the mustiness of stale air that seems to propagate in confinement, becoming heavier, thicker with each lonely day. They need to be aired out; they need sunlight, just like me. My mother and I speak on the phone, I reassure her that I'm all right and to stop worrying.

My feet find their way onto the cobblestones of Old Town, where I once walked hand-in-hand with the one I loved. Everything in those days was taken for granted: the setting, the weather, the one beside me. It's all still here, minus the key ingredient. I have plenty of regret in my life: friends I could've made, places I should've traveled, experiences I missed out on. But nothing is more regretful than the way I lost her.

I wonder where she is, who she is with, whose bubble she is filling. Mine has certainly deflated without her breath. It doesn't seem true, but I tried to make it work with her following Dusty's death. For weeks, I listened to the encouraging, reassuring messages she would say, but nothing made it easier to swallow. No combination of well-placed words could dull the pain. That might be when I stopped listening to her, when I stopped noticing her.

I wish I could take it all back—all the horrible things I said, all the terrible ways I treated her. Even though we'd been together for a year, we hadn't been through anything traumatic, nothing to test or reinforce our bond. Only bright, sunny days. This blessing became our curse, because when the hard times came, we had no foundation to lean upon–from honeymoon to Armageddon in a single morning. I know it's my own fault; I pushed away the person that actually loved me because the other person I loved left. I can't seem to forgive myself. I can't seem to stop hating myself. It seems that I received my wish after all. I was tested by life and I failed.

I want to be a better person. I want to get her back. I want to stop drinking. But the clock has struck 6 p.m. and my hands are shaking. I shove my palms into my pockets, feeling them vibrate as if bitten by hypothermia. My forehead is buttered with sweat; my stomach is doing cartwheels. I know these are dire signs of my declining health, but all I can think of is drinking. A single drink to take these feelings away. A little sip to wash these thoughts away.

Maybe that's why they call it *spirits*—because they possess you.

## 10

Tonight, the pinwheel landed on tequila. I've exhausted the majority of booze selections and reluctantly landed on the panty-dropper. I've never cared for the worm-infested liquor, but at least I bought some limes. Like a proper sous-chef, I retrieve a white cardboard bottle of table salt from the littered cupboard. After slicing the slightly overripe limes, I set up a shooter.

Dab of salt between the thumb and index finger, slice of lime between those two digits, and the glass in the other hand. Lick, gulp, suck. "How *genius*. I'd like to meet the damn legend that came up with this bit of ingenuity." Lick, gulp, suck. "Sir, Ma'am, you may be an unsung hero to the rest of 'em, but tonight I sing your praises!"

Lick, gulp, suck, slam. *Could be the closed captioning of a porn.*

The transparent bottle is creeping below the halfway mark, and I don't feel a thing. *Building up that tolerance.* I light a cigarette and flip the switch to the oven exhaust fan. The swirling smoke dances along to the background music. I'm not sure when the smoking began, but when I discovered there is nothing better than a long drag after a harsh pull, there was no going back. After two puffs of the menthol-laced tobacco, the liquor is triggered, activated. That nauseous, dizzy, yet exhilarating sensation drips from forehead to fingertip.

I'm drunk—on the cusp of shit-faced—barreling toward blackout.

Dead men sing through my stereo while I stare at the shortened, Halloween-orange tip of a burning cigarette. The end smolders, flakes, and grays between my knuckles. My fingernails show a new hint of yellow—the same hue as the used-up filter. The smoke keeps time to the tune before vanishing into the vacuum.

Lyrics have always fascinated me. Hidden meanings, secret codes, inside jokes. These concoctions of words are sung along to at stadiums, belted out in traffic, and written on cheap t-shirts. But the phrases are reborn after the composer passes away; an additional layer of mystery is injected into each hook and riff. *Everything* is more analyzed after people die. What did they mean by this? Were they trying to tell us something?

I find myself wondering about that sort of thing since I left Dusty's house.

Lick, gulp, suck, drag.

How you die—not necessarily the way you live—determines how you're remembered. A person could be a selfish, thieving, asshole their entire life, but if they sacrifice themselves to save another, they're forever remembered as a hero. On the contrary, someone could live a remarkable life, then take their own and/or someone else's life, and be forever remembered as a villain.

I wonder how *I'll* be remembered. I haven't been

overwhelmingly loved *or* hated, always right down the middle of the road. Nice enough to get along with everybody on the surface, but never brazen or confident enough to take a stand and make a few enemies–besides Luna, but I'm not sure what that was.

Lick, gulp, drag.

*What will people say as my body rots beneath the soil? Will anyone cry? Will anyone care? And will anyone miss me?*

With every isolated moment, I separate further from the outside world and burrow deeper within my own thoughts.

Sometimes I wonder what it's like to die. It's a natural thought, but I've been thinking about it an unnatural amount lately. If done properly, as in Dusty's case, BAM, you're gone–didn't even hear the gunshot. One minute you're seated comfortably on your bed, an oil-coated barrel rested against your incisors, and then nothing.

*Do you go to sleep?*

I guess it just ends. Maybe it's like not remembering anything before you're born. You're suddenly lost in a dreamless, thoughtless sleep. All the problems of the physical world are washed away with buckshot.

I wonder which is better: to know death is coming to your door or to be taken without warning. On the one hand, you could say your goodbyes and at least live life to the fullest before leaving. God knows that nobody actually starts to live until they know they're dying. But that anticipation—the damned anticipation—would sour every half-sweet moment. A cruel monster plucking away at your brain, planted inside, its sole purpose to remind you of what is coming, that it's all too little too late. The constant reassurance that your death will shatter every person you love. Tucked beneath every smile is pain, every laugh is a scream, every word is a eulogy.

On the other hand, maybe I'd prefer not to know.

Mostly, I think about the gun Dusty used—its powder-coated exterior, its kitchen-cabinet brown stock. A steady face instructing a trembling hand to chamber a red shell, thumbing the brass ends into the magazine one by one. Filling it to capacity just for the final audible satisfaction of the rounds seating properly inside, even though only one will be chosen. Finding their homes, waiting patiently for their order, each shell hoping to get a slap on the ass.

I should've taken it out of his hands—the last thing he ever held—felt its warmth, understanding of its innocence being merely a tool. Unbiased, at the will of its wielder.

Gulp, drag.

Other times, I wonder if I'm *already* dead. I pried the barrel from his gnarled, rigor mortis grip, pumped the ribbed fore-end, and pressed its pointed sight against the thin skin beneath my chin.

I can see it all happening.

My thumb engages the crescent moon trigger, the round is struck, and the fragmented explosion barrels toward me like an unstoppable missile launch.

Impact.

The shotgun shell acts as a needle against a birthday balloon, applying a second coat of fresh organic matter throughout the bedroom, cutting in what the first coat missed.

Two bodies were found inside that room–beheaded fraternal twins.

Maybe this *is* death. How the hell should I know?

But that can't be. Even though I've had these suicidal thoughts, I could never do that to my family. They are the burden that has kept me alive. But am I even *me* anymore? I'm all too aware that I became a different person that day—forever changed. The elasticity of my facial features hardened to stone; my view of the world defiled.

The fragments should have stopped with him. The ceiling drywall should've caught them all. But they didn't stop; they continue to travel, viciously cutting through the tranquil air of life to destroy everything in their path.

If it is true, if I *am* dead, I don't regret it.

Gulp.

That last drink summons a thick fog at the foot of my vision. It rolls forth, billowing as if controlled by some robed sorceress. The smoke sweeps about the ground, expanding into the atmosphere, slowly pinching my sight to a veiled pinpoint. I attempt to brush the fumes away with a quick shake of my head, but the sudden movement provokes my entire body to sway.

My sweaty palms attempt to stabilize my wavering body, but they fail, slipping from the gritty surface and leaving a finger-streaked trail of stovetop. My hands reach for the oven handlebar, my grip locking as the world tilts on its axis.

The oven door swings open. The lights go out.

My eyes burst open on the kitchen floor. I can't breathe through my nose. I can't breathe through my mouth. Everything is clogged, backed up.

Choked.

Tears are streaming down the sides of my sinking face, pooling into my ear canals. White spots and bright fireworks flash over my vision. My mouth is wide open, yet I can't pull a breath. My pounding head feels trapped underwater, searching for the surface as the pressure mounts, becoming more desperate and frantic with each suffocating second. I lie on my back, my arms flopping on the floor, a pair of disoriented beached fish.

I'm *not* underwater, but my mouth is full of liquid.

I attempt to swallow, but the valves malfunction. My stomach swells and elevates with such heights that I can see its bulge through my bottom, cell-door eyelashes. My right hand reaches into my mouth to scoop the invisible water as my cloudy eyes begin to fail. The index finger makes it inside, digging into a hot, chunky pool of mud filled to the corners of my gaping lips. A reservoir of magma boils against my tonsils. My breathless spasms send bubbles to the surface, popping and spraying noxious debris onto my streaked cheeks.

I grab my lower jaw and throw my head to the right. Gravity pulls the substance toward the floor, and an abrupt cough scatters black vomit across the linoleum. My abdomen deflates, vacuuming to my rib cage. I cannot stop coughing, heaving, and vomiting.

My stomach is being rung out like a dirty sponge, the tired organ twisting and pulling in every conceivable direction to expel each drop of filth.

While I *am* alive after all, I may not be for much longer. While curled in the fetal position, heaving until my veins are ripe to pop, I decide I want to live. *Please, let me make it through this. I'm done. I don't want to wind up like Dusty. I don't want to be found blue-faced, buried in my own excrement.* What a terrible way to die. Choking. Suffocating. Suffering.

The heaving fit ceases, as one more cough would be certain to kill me. I lie there on my side, inhaling deep breaths, filling my lungs with invisible energy, and staring into the opened mouth of the stove with bloodshot eyes. Its crumb-baked bulb softly illuminates the image of a new life in my mind.

Lying perfectly still, I smile amongst the sewage.

## 11

*I almost died last night.* Deceased by unintentional suicide, yet suicide all the same. Drinking myself to death, choking on my own bile as the acidity chomps through the tooth enamel. What if I hadn't woken up? What if I couldn't have turned my head? How pathetic it is to imagine the expressionless paramedics finding me after days—or weeks—of me being dead on the floor.

Rotting away, decaying.

Tiny, creepy-crawly pests traveling from miles away, squeezing through cracks in the floorboards to feast on my flesh. All the insects marching in a straight line, so polite, so well-mannered. *No pushing or shoving; there's plenty to go around.* Their needle teeth and spindly legs swarm my body. So much motion that it appears I could be alive, moving. Their legs tickle, their teeth pinch. An insatiable itch you can't scratch—because you're dead.

I haven't physically interacted with anyone besides the liquor store clerk for weeks. My absence wouldn't be noticed. Maybe the smell would've given it away. My neighbor beating on the door, screaming for me to take out the trash. This persistent, pesky neighbor waits a day or more between visits. All while I decompose.

She resorts to rubbing fragrant hand lotion on her

upper lip.

With the smell worsening, she'd be forced to address the issue with the landlord. My sweet, old landlord would make a special appointment to come and use her master key to open my front door, her innocent soul suspecting her property is simply abandoned. Her tired eyes peer through smudged, horn-rimmed glasses, thinking, *Someone's not getting their security deposit back.* Never anticipating the mess within.

What a horrible way to be remembered: the man who choked to death on tequila vomit, alone in his dilapidated rental. Worse yet, no one even cared to notice. Not to mention that I *knew* this would happen. I knew that every night I passed out on that floor that could be it. I didn't care, but now my stomach churns at my own sickening memories.

Self-mutilation doesn't always leave physical scars.

Suicide is a contagious, rotten disease. Trauma breeds trauma. Suicide propagates suicide.

Depressed thoughts weave into a singular strand of rope, and with each perceived negative experience, a knot is tied–each mistakenly linked together until a net is formed with the soul writhing within.

Not me. I won't do that to my family. I won't be responsible for haunting someone else's life—not like Dusty. I know what it's like to be left behind. I may not respect myself, but at least I still care about others.

I spend the following day cleaning my apartment, including my plumbing, as I pour the harsh liquor into the sink basin. The cold sweats amplify the shakiness, aggravation, and the nauseous internal storm. Every symptom tempts me to have a drink, to feel better in an instant. But I remain determined as I watch the mini alcohol tornado swirl down the drain.

I'm getting out of this place. Time for a fresh start.

## 12

I've met someone. The two of us fit like a needle to the groove. Her name is Annabelle, and we met in the most unlikely place I ever imagined: Alcoholics Anonymous. She is fantastic, a wholesome person who can relate to my current situation. She is beautiful, articulate, and as gentle as a hummingbird. It was as if we were magnetized to one another when I took those first hesitant steps into the basement meeting.

Her eyes snatched the breath from my lips. They were green and magnificent. They reminded me of Luna. I was afraid I had forgotten what her eyes looked like in person, that the memory would fade a little more with each day until there was nothing left. But as soon as I saw Anna, I knew I'd never need to worry—some things are impossible to forget.

I could feel those eyes on my pale skin during that first meeting, never breaking her stare and softly smiling when I'd glance her way. I could sense that she understood my suffering. When the white-haired leader asked, "*Who'd like to be Arden's sponsor?*" Anna's hand nearly burst through the tiled ceiling. That gesture meant the world to me; I felt so welcomed and wanted, even though I didn't feel worthy. But for some reason, she sought me out, bringing warmth into the coldest period of my life. I would've never guessed by looking at her, but she hit bottom a couple years ago and managed to pull herself from the abyss.

We began spending all of our free time together, quickly becoming inseparable best friends. I knew that she wanted more than friendship, and I was attracted to her, too, but my mind was still consumed with Luna. I had to remind myself that this *was* Anna and not Luna, because while looking into her identical eyes, it's hard to tell the difference. Sometimes I got the odd feeling that Luna was watching me through Anna's eyes.

Well, until I discovered Luna had started dating someone. When I searched her online, I wasn't surprised to see her smiling face beside another man in her profile picture–that same smile that was once neighbor to mine. Even though it was anticipated, it hurt all the same—an invisible fist rearranging my guts. She was the woman I was supposed to marry. But there are no signed contracts. She pulled out before we sealed the deal. I'm happy for her, though, and last I heard, they're getting serious. Maybe I didn't mean that much to her, just a cracked speed bump in the road, only serving to slow her down before she arrived at the destination.

Nothing is worse than overestimating your role in a loved one's life.

I have no right to complain. I blew my chance with her. I had it all such a short time ago; it feels like yesterday that I was the wealthiest man alive. But I must continue moving forward. I know that after my kitchen floor wake-up call.

For the most part, I'm happier than I've been in a long time. Anna and I have progressed into a romantic relationship, I'm building beautiful houses at a large construction firm, and I'm sober after weeks of being sewn into my bed with a bucket on the floor.

I've dated Anna for two months, and she is a far better woman than I deserve. I'm grateful for her in my life. I want to move on, but the bobby pins won't allow me to forget.

They are everywhere; it seems like they *find* me.

Last week, we had a date night at the movies. Annabelle and I arrived early and had our choice of any seat in the house. We ran through the empty theater aisles, her cardinal-red hair swaying the opposite direction of each step she took. We stopped at two random chairs, each of us sitting down, full of breathless giggles. As I passed her a thin box of candy, something caught my eye on the floor. A perfect bobby pin was positioned between my shoes, as if it were meant for me. I remained frozen the entire film, unable to move my feet or thoughts away from the object.

The pins arrive when my mind begins to move on—always when I'm least expecting, vulnerable. A couple days ago, I went to the dentist, and there it was beside the sign-in sheet. The same one I once found in our home. The same ones I'd watch Luna pick from her hair. Waiting for me, reminding me. They are everywhere, always in places they shouldn't be: wedged in sidewalk cracks, lying on bus seats, even at my new construction job. I don't look for them. In fact, I dread finding them. It's a tease, but just like Anna's eyes, it seems Luna is somehow communicating with me, looking into my eyes through the wavy, blackened metal. Keeping watch over my life, making sure I'm happy, but also ensuring I don't forget.

Even when I'm not mentally terrorized by the mysterious hairpins, the actors from my past pick up the slack. I run into mutual friends from when Luna and I were together. They *know* we've started dating other people, but like a cooped-up dog seeing the mail truck rolling down the street, they can't help but bark uncontrollably. These people constantly update me on how Luna is, what she is doing—even when I don't ask or wish to know.

Why are you forever associated with those you date? Maybe the two of us became one in other people's minds. Now, when they see the one without the other, it appears odd to their minds. We aren't whole in their eyes, half of the picture is missing, and most days I wouldn't disagree.

"Good evening, friends," Dan, the lanky, white-haired AA speaker says from the front of the meeting room. "Before we begin, I'd like to take a moment to discuss an exciting opportunity offered by our gracious hosts. First Baptist Church is looking for volunteers to attend a three-week mission trip that will depart for Peru next week. They understand this is short notice, but they've had a few members drop out last minute for unspecified reasons. Membership in the congregation is *not* necessary to participate, and all expenses are paid. The mission is to help construct a new church in the country and spread their positive message to the community. If anyone is interested, especially those with construction experience, please see me after the meeting. Now, who would like to share first?" Dan refolds the creased pamphlet and tucks it into his back pocket.

"I think you should go," Annabelle whispers in my ear.

I've never been out of the country, and I'm not necessarily religious; this doesn't sound up my alley.

"I think you need this," she says, her cool breath laced with menthol.

"I wouldn't be able to get the time off; I just started at my job," I argue with minimal breath.

Anna leans close. "Isn't your boss a member of this church? I'm sure he would be ecstatic to see you go."

*It does seem like a good opportunity, and maybe it would be good for me.*

I spend the entire meeting racing inside my mind as the others spill their souls onto the bare concrete floor. While debating the huge decision and weighing the potential consequences, members begin to fold up their chairs. The screeching metal swirls inside the tiny, cinder-block room, signaling the meeting is finished.

"Let's go talk to him."

I touch her delicate wrist with the tip of my outstretched finger. "I don't want to go."

She places her hand on mine. "I know you don't, but you *need* to."

Moments later, Dan is speaking to the pastor, spelling out my information and committing me to this choice. I watch as his mouth stretches and compresses inside a rounded grouping of snowy facial hair. I'm sick with nervousness, nausea, and excitement.

As our shoes glide to the double doors, I grab hold of Anna's soft hand. "Thank you."

## 13

Peru is magnificent and is not in need of my help. The mountains are pages from a fairy tale, the people are sweeter than fresh-squeezed guava, and despite the unforgiving heat, I love it here.

Surprisingly enough, I've taken on somewhat of a lead role in the church's construction, and things are coming along well. It seems that those years spent working construction have finally paid off.

Although I'm still not a religious man, I've felt a change within myself during the past two weeks. It's hard *not* to feel close to God when performing this work. The villagers treat us like heroes, always smiling, always happy to see us. I've even made friends with a group of kids. They taught me how to play soccer, and I taught them how to drive a nail.

The scenery is breathtaking, the food is delicious, the culture is rich, but the joy our presence has brought surpasses it all.

Today is a scheduled day off for the team, but as I wander through town, my feet lead me to the church. I stand outside, admiring the fresh structure: its textured white walls, thick-paned glass windows, and a dramatic peak above its wooden front door. My mind contemplates what this building represents and how much it will be valued for generations to come. The lives that will be celebrated here, the many people that will depend on its doctrine for constant strength in the hardest of times, the lives it will mourn. It's a simplistic design without any frills, built only as a place of worship and shelter. I like that.

I always thought that if I *was* religious, I would start my own church. Only, it would be slightly different, as there would be no building, structure, or icons. The gathering would take place in a forest clearing, the path to the opening unmarked but well-worn by the willful members' soles. The pews would be flattened, fallen logs, the curved bark gently scratching against the back of each person's calves until it's worn away, leaving unique sets of ghost legs against the wood grain to mark a person's favorite seat. I would keep my sermons brief, breathing my fleeting message and allowing nature to fill in the blanks. The brooding trees remain fearful of public speaking until the reassuring breeze gives them the courage to whisper. Wildlife would occasionally roam through the service; a majestic deer or unsuspecting fox would encounter our group as each of us remain still, just content with the moment, witnessing God through the eyes of His creations. There would be no cancellations; the service would be held in rain or shine, because *all* weather is a gift. I would permit anyone to speak or stay silent. I wouldn't be in charge. We wouldn't require anything, no donation baskets would be passed, and no one would be guilted into volunteering for extra duties on the weekend. There would be a single purpose to this mission: to pause your black-and-white life and appreciate the plethora of color surrounding you.

"Excuse me?" A churning voice brings me back to reality.

"Yes, sorry. I was daydreaming a bit," I say, recounting my fantasy and hoping it doesn't sound too *cultish.*

The stranger is tall with unwashed, curly hair tucked behind his ears. "You're helping build this church, aren't you?"

"Yes, for another couple days."

"You're doing a bang up job. It's really come together in the past couple weeks." His white teeth sparkle from behind his thick beard.

"Thanks, it's been great. I haven't seen you around town; my name's Arden," I say as we shake hands.

"Pleasure, Arden. I'm Jason, but call me Jay."

I thought I was getting tan on this trip, but compared to Jay's darkened skin, it looks like I've never *seen* the sun.

My thumbs hook into my belt loops. "Are you on a mission trip, too?"

"In a sense. I'm heading up a dig in the mountains, hoping to find something good this time." He motions to the left.

"Digging for what?" My eyebrows furrow.

"*Anything* at this point. My team and I haven't had much luck this past month. Today's our last day before we catch a plane back to the States. But unfortunately the saying is right: you win some, you lose some." His shoulders lightly shrug with disappointment.

"That's incredible, Jay. Even though you haven't found anything, I hope you're enjoying yourself all the same. I take it you're an archaeologist?"

"Guilty as charged."

"It's hard for me to feel sorry for you—you're working my dream job," I reply, embarrassed by the sound of my voice, at cutting myself open in front of this complete stranger, feeling the green jealousy seep from my pores.

He flicks his head dramatically to the rear, a lock of hair falling free from his ear's constraint. "No kidding? Well, if you've got some free time, I could always use an extra set of hands."

My eyes widen, and excitement veils my vision. "Are you serious?"

His lips playfully slant downward. "Why not? But before you start pressing against your zipper, this has to be off the books. I can't pay you; this trip's account went *bone* dry last week."

My head bobbles from side to side with the rubbernecked grace of an infant. "That's no problem.

When do we leave?"

He claps his rough hands. "Where do you think I was heading?"

Ten minutes later, I'm on an archaeological dig—in Peru. *This is insane.* I work alongside twenty other men, mostly Peruvian, with a healthy mix of Americans. Everyone is friendly, but brief, as their deep tans camouflage them into the forest. They remove their ball-caps to wipe their brows with a dirty forearm, flicking their hat toward me in a silent greeting. Their shovels take mouthful bites from the earth, their expressions filled with exhaustion and worn spirits. Mine is the opposite. I cannot contain my ear-to-ear smile as my weathered tools scrape the soil. I can't believe this is my life.

I peer around my work area to see giant trees with bases resembling webbed feet. The roots are spilled and scattered across the soil, overlapping and interwoven with one another, giant boulders are entombed in their grasp. In the seconds between the racket of tools, I can hear a distant gushing waterfall. There is a sweetness in the air, a pureness—the way the earth was meant to smell.

After three hours, the sun's invisible fists are pounding on my back. My relentless perspiration is indecisive on whether to remain a liquid or vapor. No one is talking. The only sounds are the sifting of dirt and the abused tools carving trenches. I was only given a hasty introduction to these men, but I feel a closeness to them as each of us work toward a common goal: finding something, *anything* left behind by our forgotten ancestors.

I've pried countless rocks inside my area, each time hoping there is some abandoned treasure buried underneath, but there was a multi-colored snake instead. Jay rushed over and jumped inside the hole, quickly snatching the animal from its freshly exposed hiding place. Funny thing was, I didn't scream; I didn't know *what* to do as I stood frozen with the dust-caked shovel against my chest. He pinned and grabbed the animal from behind its head, lifting its long, dangling body that never seemed to stop uncoiling.

"Close call. You *do not* want to get bitten by one of these bastards; she's venomous. Shit, even if a snake's not deadly, you're still bound to get a nasty infection. Nobody taught these bastards how to brush their teeth." Jay holds the snake as he casually speaks, the other workers barely taking notice. Its pitchforked maroon tongue flicks from between its jaws, its heavy body flexing, brushing against Jay's cargo pant leg. "Gonna go toss her in the forest. Our contract states that we can't kill anything, even something that would happily kill us. This is an environmentally protected area and we're lucky enough to have the permission to dig here. We want to stay on the government's good side." With his free hand, he climbs from the hole as the snake's pencil-tipped tail jots cursive in the soil.

The sun's intensity is lessening as the day winds down.

The colors it paints against the sky's canvas are breathtaking: red, orange, yellow, purple, pink–each blended masterfully into the next, making it impossible to determine where one begins and one ends. They have become one.

Although I'm having the time of my life, nothing has been found, and I begin to feel sorrow for Jay. I lean on my shovel and peer from my hole as he makes rounds to the workers, somehow remaining positive enough to provide encouragement, struggling to keep his own failing spirit alive, knowing the clock has all but expired on his once-promising expedition. The dream is slowly dying before his eyes. Still, he offers a reassuring smile in grim circumstances, each man looking to him for unwavering direction in the darkest hour—the embodiment of a true leader.

My shovel-head attempts to pry a large rock in my path, wobbling its weight back and forth, slowly loosening the earth's prehistoric grip. Tiny, confetti sparks fly as the curved metal scrapes against the enormous boulder. I drop the shovel to the soil, opting to dig my fingers into the widening creases, putting all my weight behind each labored pull. Every inch of my shirt is stuck to my body, the fabric multiple shades darker since the start of the day. My hooked hands clench to its rough edges; my back muscles stretch and strain with every bit of reserved energy at their disposal. I tighten my grip and give one final heave.

The boulder suddenly pops free, sending me falling

onto my backside with the rock graciously pausing against my shoe soles. A tacky cloud kicks up, obscuring my little jungle pit. I'm lost in the dust, and the shrouded vision causes me to panic as the memory of the coiled snake flashes in my memory. Maybe not just one this time, maybe a *hundred* snakes, each one desperate to slither through the bottom of my gaping pant leg. The countless pairs of slatted eyes directed into mine, their flickering, split tongues tasting my scent in the air.

Thick, garden hose clones.

My pant leg is spread open as a promising habitat for an opportunist creature in search of survival—an invitation that offers warmth, shelter, and food. I feel one enter, but only slightly—a hint. When it passes the top of my sagging sock, that's when I really feel it, right up against the shinbone, moving freely, naturally. Its cold-blooded body slithers with slow, calculated movements up toward my knee and finds a roadblock of pinched denim. The veteran explorer shifts its path to the back of my leg. It careens along the rear of my knee and up my frantically twitching hamstring. The invitation extends to its friends who follow suit, penetrating every opening. They crisscross along my stomach, brushing against my chest; they pour from my shirt sleeves.

I feel every mouth open. Long, needled teeth hang in curved bows, dripping with venom. Their unhinged jaws designed to feed on larger prey, always aiming to fit as much as they can. A million shadows begin to fall.

The dust clears as I claw at my legs and arms inside the hole, yet the only reptiles in sight are inside my mind.

*Thank God, but...I do see something.*

When my heart finally settles, I see a round object. It's much smoother than any rock I've come across. Something is different about this shape; it's blatantly alien to this lifeless world. I crawl on worn-out hands and kneel before the object, reaching my blistered digits around its edges. It gently falls into my hands, and I know this is no stone. I can identify faint geometric designs through the caked soil, and just as one peers into the nighttime sky, the longer I look, the more I see—colors, shapes, animals, the depictions are too much to comprehend.

My voice falters because there are no words. I've found something. This is the moment I've dreamed of since I was a child. I don't even know what the object is, but it doesn't matter. This moment is better than I conceived, than I could've ever wished for.

A lifetime ago, I was on a porch repairing those broken boards with the unlikely man who'd become my best friend. His reassuring words filling me with pride and happiness. He was such a good man, my hurt and anger never allowed me to miss him, but now I know that I do. I miss him dearly.

The repressed emotions come rushing in—the friend who left, the woman I left.

Someone whistles. "Arden, my man! He's got something over here!" Black clouds fall on me inside the hole, blocking out the afternoon sun, blanketing me in inky shade. Voices gather above, each offering congratulations while debating the artifact's identity. None of it matters. I remain glued to the object in my hands, unable to take my glinting eyes from it.

I've unearthed more than a simple artifact. I've excavated my purpose.

## 14

**"I**'m sorry, I can't do this anymore." The sounds leave my lips. I attempt to reel them back in through the air, but it's too late. The damaging syllables careen toward the unsuspecting target, slicing through the atmosphere of her one-bedroom apartment, impaling her with the barbed weaponry. Annabelle stands before me, wounded, shifting in her shoes. Her fingertips roll and compact a burnt cigarette filter to a point.

The pain in her eyes is reminiscent of a doe I saw a lifetime ago.

I was traveling northbound, my cluttered mind recounting the unimportant events of the day, analyzing trivial conversations, dwelling on the problems of tomorrow, entirely too consumed with others' opinions of me. The traffic on the southbound lane was stopped ahead. Our lanes slowed as well, each person overly cautious and hesitant to the unknown danger, each passerby expecting to gawk at a fender-bender, maybe an overturned tractor-trailer, something our minds were familiar with.

If only.

Positioned in front of those hundreds of idling vehicles was a doe. She was lying perfectly still in the center lane, her broken legs tucked underneath her beige torso. The creature's bristly hair laid unnaturally on the hot pavement, far from the safety of the shady trees. A dented car stood at arm's length from the animal, its passengers huddled near—children were crying in the median. It felt like I was passing through the eye of a hurricane–so much stimuli, so much heartbreak. Each red-eyed person unsure of what to do, neither deer nor person prepared for their paths to cross. An unfair, cruel twist had been thrown into their daily plans.

I was able to look into the deer's eyes as my wheels crept by. They were sad eyes, but accepting of her fate. She stared into the distance, seemingly separated from the current situation. She wasn't afraid; she wasn't weeping from the pain; she knew it was her time. Maybe her thoughts were filled with visions of her children and how they must go on without her. Or perhaps she was contemplating a lifetime of freedom coming to an end, dreaming of the forest, the magical place where falling fruit acts as a dinner bell to every hungry creature and where graceful, orange butterflies exchange kisses in mid-air.

My vehicle was forced to keep moving, my whimpering soul crushed by the inability to turn back the wheels of time. This moment occurred years ago, but her glance has forever lingered inside my memory. I can only imagine the everlasting impact it had on the driver.

"I learned a lot in Peru. I want to do something more with my life. I want to prove myself wrong about everything I've ever believed. I want to be fulfilled. I can't give a half-hearted effort any longer—not to my job, not to my beliefs, and not to you. You deserve better than what I'm giving you. There are moments in my life that I simply can't move past, but I must learn to live with them. You're the best thing that has happened to me in a long time, and I do have love for you. But I still have love for another, and that will never change. I can't be with her either, but you shouldn't be anybody's second choice, including mine."

I've never spoken to Anna about Luna, never opened that chapter of my life to her, even though I have told her about other, far less meaningful exes of my past. It's an unspoken truth, but even *I* know there are different levels of ex-lovers. No relationship is an exception; there's always that *one* ex that, no matter how long you may be married, you'd never trust your spouse to be alone with that person. Not after thirty, forty, or a hundred happy, faithful years; not after five kids; not after battling a disease. The anti-hero from your lover's previous life. The haunting apparition that looms over each argument, every private peek into their search history, every personal insecurity. Nothing could convince you to trust the two of them together, even for a moment. You fear their ancient bond—although weathered by the years—still possesses enough strength to break your own.

A dying fire can always be rekindled if the coals are still warm enough.

Anna attempts to conceal a translucent tear against her speckled cheek. The drop magnifies each freckle as it passes. "I knew this would happen. I knew that by pushing you to go on that trip that I might lose you. But it was a sacrifice I had to make for you to find yourself. I'm sad to see you go, but I'm glad you're leaving better than when I found you."

"It kills me to do this to you." I speak these words into Anna's eyes, yet I could be saying it to Luna.

"It's my womanly duty to lie, to stay strong in front of you, but I can't...it's killing me, too."

"I'm so sorry, Anna. You mean the world to me. I hope you can forgive me."

It's Luna all over again—the same eyes, the same tears, the same tragic ending. I'm doomed to break every heart that loves me.

We hug and I breathe her in for the final time, her hair entwined with scents of passion fruit and smoke. Our arms loosen their grips, each pulling away from one another, the remnants of her sadness soaked into my collar.

Then she is gone. The most important person in my life vanishes, her job complete. I'm sickened at my own decision as I remain stationary, brimming with regret. I've given this moment tremendous thought over the past week but never desired to go through with it.

I know it was the right thing to do, and she also felt it when she'd catch me glancing toward an opening restaurant door, always eager to see who may be walking through. Never offering Anna my undivided attention, my mind always partially adrift, my wandering gaze pulling taut against its leash.

Even though Luna is now happily married, I always felt somehow guilty being with Annabelle. As if I were cheating on Luna, like we never broke up.

Relationships are like homes. Some are well constructed, the builders forgoing no expense, using only the best workers and finest materials. Others are thrown together with little care, a cookie cutter home from a lackadaisical builder just looking to make a buck. Some can weather a thousand brutal storms without a flinch, standing tall in the face of unprecedented events, the impenetrable structure rooted to the earth. Others collapse at the first glimpse of a darkened cloud.

Some homes can stand abandoned in the forest for years, or even decades, as the destructive elements take their toll. Corrosive water decapitates every screw head; a pneumatic crowbar peels the roof back like a sardine lid; the shutters dangle as hangnails; the tilted chandelier sprouts a thick, ginger beard of rust; the soil shifts to create an inlaid staircase walking up the foundation. Uncared for, unloved, caked with thick mildew and black mold—yet patiently awaiting the day of their owner's return.

If I can't be with her, I'll be alone. I refuse to settle in this world any longer. I'm no longer content to thumb through life's pages, speed-reading, so eager to reach the end. I'm tired of never appreciating the tiny intricacies and shaping moments. The story within itself. My entire life changed the moment that artifact was freed from the earth. There was no going back to the way things once were.

I'm devoting full attention to my own life. I want it all and nothing less.

## 15

Today marks the tenth anniversary. Ten years ago, the best friend I ever had took his own life. It's hard to believe it's been so long; the vivid memory has remained painfully fresh throughout the years. The faceless projectionist inside my memory switches on the somber machine at the moment someone mentions carpentry, chewing tobacco, or suicide. So much has evolved in my life, but that awful day has remained unchanged, preserved. An artifact buried beneath layers of soil, frozen in time.

I've accomplished much since then—more than I ever imagined. Shortly after the Peru trip, I quit my job to dedicate every moment to schooling. That first year was miserable, overlapping difficult courses, having zero social life, and living on coffee and noodles. But when I read my name on that fancy sheet of eggshell paper, I was hooked.

A grueling year later, I had a graduate degree in hand.

Even though I never dreamed of earning a Master's degree, I still craved more. Now, I'm nearly finished with an archaeological doctoral program. *Me*, the guy who was lying on a vomit-riddled floor not so long ago, is on his way to becoming a doctor.

My life accelerated following the breakup with Annabelle, and I've barely slowed along the way to look back. I've kept true to my word and haven't grown serious with anyone. This was mostly intentional, but partly because I haven't met anyone who has captivated my interest. The incredible women of my past have raised the bar to an unreachable height. The personal freedom has permitted the time and energy to focus upon education and achieving my goals, but the main goal was to become a better person, and I think I'm closer than ever.

Luna visits my dreams most nights, and despite being apart for years, it feels as though we've never lost touch. The hazy, sleep-realm encounters are heavenly, even though we rarely speak.

Each night, I'm carried away into that magical place that nobody truly understands. Some say that it's only a subconscious manifestation of our waking world, except all jumbled like the memories were tossed in a blender. Others speculate that our minds create these nighttime journeys to help us *practice* scenarios in our dreams to work out physical stresses and issues. Some say that when we dream, we enter a world beyond our current scientific or spiritual reasoning. Our soul exits our body for a stroll in the city—an astral world where it returns after our flesh dies. A world of endless possibility.

Regardless of which theory is correct, I see her with more clarity than ever before. The sensations of her presence are foreign, indescribable. I've never felt such emotions in my waking life. I'm whole in these nocturnal moments, never wanting to wake. We are simply together, we are one. I crave this self-manufactured fiction but dread it all the same. The dreams are a cruel tease, akin to hooking a $100 bill to the end of a fishing line and watching pedestrians make fools out of themselves. The clumsy people chasing the flying bill as the giggling antagonist reels in the paper bait. The climactic moment of sheer disappointment when they know they've been duped— me when I awaken.

I have the world before me these days, more than I could ever ask for, but that part of myself will forever remain empty without her to fill it. I stopped checking her online profile after she married. It's something I've learned to live with. I'm sure there are countless people going through life with similar struggles, walking down the street holding hands with their spouse, yet daydreaming of another's palm within theirs.

My new life doesn't permit me to stand still; working as a museum curator takes me to the farthest reaches of the world. My job is to find the rarest of items in the most luxurious and desolate places on the planet. With each region I venture to, I'm reminded of how massive, mysterious, and beautiful our world truly is. These same reasons once intimidated me about traveling. Now I kick myself for waiting this long. I often contemplate all the things I've missed.

This is a fresh, exciting life I've built, but there always seems to be something holding me back from being complete. It doesn't help that the bobby pins have never stopped following me. They find me in every corner of the Earth. The same bobby pins in Turkey,

China, Argentina, Germany, you name it. I find them so often it's as if I'm dropping them out of my own pockets, breadcrumbs to find my way back.

Three years ago, I gave in and started collecting them. I was in Cairo and had just witnessed the wonder of the Giza Pyramids, fulfilling a personal lifelong dream to witness them in person. Being a historical worker, I was granted special access and was able to see additional sites beyond the red, braided tourist ropes. I found myself alone in a great tomb, surrounded by thousands of ancient hieroglyphics and a giant, golden sarcophagus. The intricacies and preservation left me breathless—thousands of years of wonder, thousands to come. Every direction I turned showcased a miracle beyond comprehension, surpassing every expectation. It was the greatest day of my life.

I stood inside the tomb, soaking in the silence and filling my lungs with the ancient air. At that moment, I was thankful I'd lived through the many struggles and had never given in to the dark temptations. I was content, but I wished she were by my side to share it. There's no such thing as a *perfect* moment, but this one was damn close.

I was beside myself on the bus ride back to the hotel, trying to fathom the unbelievable things I'd seen, but also dwelling on those green eyes from my past. As I peered through the dust-caked window at those triangular miracles, a black object was wedged inside the window frame. My fingertips crammed inside the crease, prying the item from its hiding place. My intestines roiled in disbelief.

It was her pin.

Now, I knew it wasn't *her* pin, but how could it get here? Why would it be in such a place, in this part of the world, positioned in the exact seat I chose? It must be a part of her somehow—a sign that, although we aren't physically together, we're never truly apart. No matter the time, no matter the distance, no matter the people who've taken our place, we're still together.

I held the bobby pin, thumbing and smoothing the light corrosion, its simple existence dwarfing the unimaginable day I'd just experienced. My previous thoughts washed away like sandy tire tracks by the desert wind. My mind was no longer filled with the lives and mysteries surrounding the ancient Egyptians, but with the sweet memory of her voice. That shooting star glance. I felt she was with me in that moment, seated beside me on that crowded bus of sweaty tourists. Each person sitting silent, lost inside the endless thoughts, trying to cement every detail into memory—seeing themselves recounting the otherworldly experience to their bright-eyed grandchildren decades in the future. Framing this moment—its sights, its sounds, its scents—for a final recollection on their future deathbed.

I loved how the pin made me feel, like I finally wasn't alone and nothing existed outside of our love. This is how I feel in my dreams, the nocturnal sensations brought to the daylight. I couldn't leave it there; I had to take it with me. After a quick glance at my surroundings, I pushed it inside my denim pocket. I could feel its warmth in there, filled with the comfort of a loved one's touch.

Although that was the first one I kept, I now have a jarful in my studio apartment bedroom. I always get strange looks from airport workers when I empty my pockets at the security gate, revealing a handful of women's hairpins. But I don't care; they are priceless souvenirs from my travels.

Each time I locate one, that creeping, French-named feeling burrows inside my mind–deja vu. The unmistakable, stop-you-in-your-tracks sensation that I've been here before, stood in this place, felt these feelings, spoke these words. Maybe it's not so mysterious after all. If our soul exists in infinite dimensions, divided into incalculable grains of scattered sand, and each of me is existing on a mirrored, identical reality, and each of *us* is connected because we are the same person, wouldn't there be a small time lag between our lives? The tiniest fraction of a millisecond between our realities that occasionally permits the next version of me to remember another's experience. Maybe it's like a ripple, continually spreading and expanding, the endless line of me pausing, contemplating the present as it slowly becomes the past.

The Egyptian pin remains in my front pocket everywhere I go. Some people carry lucky coins, some have vibrational rocks; I have a black pin. It's my own form of an AA chip, reminding me to be thankful because life may vanish at any moment—a sobering token that roots me in the present. I've told no one about this obsession and always hide the jar inside of a closet when I have company. No one would understand the pins or why my house is filled with moonflowers, and I'd be lost trying to explain it. Some things can't be explained with words. It's my own fantasy. No one else needs to know.

These pins have accompanied me on the journey to today, when I unveil my first designed exhibit. It's been the greatest challenge of my life, but today it's all worth it. I've travelled to countless countries, read endless pages, and acquired some of the rarest items on Earth.

My name is called. I rise and walk toward the podium; flashing lights dance in my vision; my heart races beneath my folded handkerchief. My throat clears before the crowd of spectators. "Good afternoon, fellow history lovers. I'd like to thank you for coming."

A tall, square-shaped box stands beside me on the stage, draped with a shiny, black cloth. I grip its edge, the projectionist bringing me back to Dusty's front yard, his body within that black rubber bag. My moist palms crinkle the fabric as icicles form on my brow. *I've come a long way to find myself here. I'm not the same person who stood on that lawn.* My fingers tighten on its wavy stitching, and I pull the drapery, unveiling a large piece of pottery housed within. Vibrant, colorful lines decorate its rounded features—

handcrafted designs and craftsmanship that have stood the test of time. It is perfectly intact, equally as beautiful as the first time I held it. Not an inch of its magnificence has been dulled by time or repetition.

I return to the podium, unable to take my eyes from the encased artifact, remembering how my life changed inside that foreign hole. My eyes trace the deep grooves of the spiral pattern on its face–black channels that swirl about its being, spinning eternally. "This vase may not look like much in comparison to the other artifacts we've accumulated. It's not the most beautiful, nor the most revealing find in history. Its existence doesn't give major insight into the lives led before us, nor does it bring us closer to unlocking the mysteries of our ancestors. But if this building caught fire, *this* would be the object I would save, because it rescued me. This was the first artifact I found, and it altered the course of my life. Without this seemingly common piece of hardened clay, I wouldn't be here. But isn't that what life is about? Acknowledging signs that have the power to change one's life, while being trivial to another? I've steered a little off topic, but I hope each of you discovers your own dirty clay pot. Don't bother looking for it; it will find you."

*It cannot be.*

As I look through the endless sea of facial features, one combination stands out from the rest. A beautiful arrangement created by the most painstaking florist. It is Luna. I pause for what seems like an eternity, my unbelieving eyes locking with her striking glance. It is just the two of us inside this crowded room, the only two people in existence. I struggle to maintain my composure as my finger digs in the space between my collar and skin. "Anyways, we've put together a fascinating exhibit for your enjoyment and enlightenment. We hope you enjoy the tour as much as we've enjoyed creating it. Thank you." I return to my seat as the crowd's applause brings this moment into reality. *They are clapping for* me, *for what I've accomplished.* This is surreal, but all I can think of is her.

Following the ceremony, I shake countless hands and thank everyone for their support. My filthy, gritty palms are craving hand sanitizer. My mind recites coherent phrases and sentences as my head swivels throughout the room. I begin to doubt that it was even her seated in the audience. Sometimes I see her in places that she is not, my emotions escalating to their boiling points, eager for an unexpected meeting with the legend from my past, so crushed when I learn it was all an oasis. My mind clings to the bittersweet memory of her, so sad that it's over, but glad that it happened.

Today isn't one of those dreaded days, though, because she is standing behind the man I'm talking to. I see her through my peripherals, yet I don't acknowledge her presence. I remain focused on the man, a typical overly excited history buff. He's telling me all about his vast, personal artifact collection, only slightly insinuating that his is superior to mine. He might as well be speaking muffled Chinese as nothing he says is getting through to me. I continue to nod while peering into his bulging eyes, crafting what I'll finally say to Luna. I've dreamed of meeting her for *years*. One would think I'd have entire conversations rehearsed, but my mind is blank. The man notices my disinterest, shakes my hand, and moves on. There is an opening before me, and she fills it perfectly.

She is a celebrity in my eyes. I'm starstruck.

It *is* Luna, but she isn't how I remember her. She has aged, matured through the years. The softness of her features has been strengthened, her surefooted posture commands attention. She's no longer the girl I once knew; she is a woman. She doesn't look how I imagined, because even the most creative mind couldn't craft something so beautiful.

"Been a long time, Arden." Her voice is as familiar as a favorite song.

"Luna! I thought I saw you in the crowd. What are you doing here? I never pegged you for a history buff." Both of us are uncomfortable with the premise of a hug but rejecting of a formal handshake.

"You've got that right. I had to see it for myself once I heard the news. I couldn't believe *you* were opening your own exhibit. I re-read the newspaper article five times." Her green eyes sparkle in the overhead lights.

"Believe me, I'm equally surprised."

"Everything looks great. You look great." The bobby pin feels warm against my thigh.

"So do you! How have you been?" I ask, forgetting that we are submerged in a crowd.

"I'm good. I know you're busy, but would you be free to meet after the event and catch up?"

This must be a dream. "Sure, I know the perfect place. You ever heard of Old Town?"

"I'll meet you in the lobby." She offers a joyful smile and disappears back into the ocean.

My mother's sweet voice echoes from decades past. "You have to give people an incentive to notice you, a reason to make you stand out amongst all the crowd. Be honest, would *you* date you?" Today, I've never been more confident to answer *yes*. I'm proud of my accomplishments, of the person I've become, of the things I've seen. I'm *standing* inside my accomplishments, surrounded by the artifacts from my travels, each expanding my personal bubble a bit more. Every person has come to see what I've built, to admire the beauty of our predecessors, and to understand their own origins. Everything about this situation excites me. It's the reason I've pulled breath for the past several years. But now it all seems trivial compared to my encounter with Luna. She's the prize I've been searching for, and once again, the treasure has found me.

I enter the lobby as the event is winding down,

watching people walk to their cars with colorful programs and souvenir bags clutched in their grips, their hands and minds heavier, their wallets lighter. My job is complete.

I stand on my tiptoes, sifting through the crowd, but she is nowhere to be seen. Maybe she decided to leave or felt reconnecting with me was a bad idea.

*I see her.* She is waiting for me, the angel from my dreams. Luna is seated next to a three-tiered, cascading fountain that marks the center of the museum. A pinprick of warming light in an ashen sky. Her radiance cutting through the haziness to remind the planet that although beauty may be temporarily masked, it will always reemerge. Seeing me, she smiles that same enchanting smile–the missing piece of my story. I'm an observer of this moment, all is right in the world, just as it was. There is no past, no future, only the present. I could stay here forever.

Luna glides toward me with a swan's fluidity. "Didn't your mother ever teach you it's rude to stare?" She opens with her animated, cocked left eyebrow. I'm transformed back to that patio, experiencing love for the first time.

"Sorry, but I *still* can't make myself look away."

She shakes her head with a bashful grin.

We walk together, our mouths hushed as our minds process this moment of time. I finally say, "I guess we were bound to run into each other at some point, but it's pretty bizarre it happened here."

"Not *that* bizarre. I've always felt we're just on the same wavelength, even when we're not."

Walking side by side with eyes pointed forward, each of us is unsure about how to behave. "Thanks so much for coming to support me. It really meant a lot to see you, especially after so many years."

"I wouldn't have missed it for the world. I couldn't be more proud of you; you've really grown," she says while nudging my arm with her pointed elbow.

"I think we can both agree that's a good thing."

"No offense, but yes." She nods her head, and I can almost see the tender memories swimming through her mind.

"What about you? Marriage, kids?" I ask, aware of the answer.

"Marriage, yes. Kids, no."

*You should have been my wife.* "Looks like we've both grown up a tad since we last spoke."

"I guess it was destined to happen sooner or later." Her delicate shoulders shrug inside of her thin, black sweater.

Our shoes meet the bumpy cobblestones from our past. I glance at the crowd as they mingle through the colorful stores and umbrella-decorated patios that frame the strip. Everything is so familiar, as if I'm thumbing through a box of old, dusty photographs in an antique store.

My feet pause abruptly. "I should say something before we become strangers for another decade."

Luna looks up at me, her plump lips pressed in a soft pout. "Sure, go ahead."

"It was all my fault, everything. I'm so sorry for what I did to you, for how I treated you–"

"Don't, please. Don't. You don't have to."

"Yes, I do—"

She presses a flat palm against my heart. "What happened between us was, for some reason, meant to happen. Dusty, us, everything. I don't know why, but I know you weren't *you* when we ended. I knew you were gone, gone far away, and I couldn't bring you back. I tried. I tried for a long time, Arden. I waited for even longer. As much as it pained me, I knew you'd have to bring *yourself* back, without my help. It appears that you did, just—"

"Not in time," I finish.

She nods. "I have a husband. His name is Casey, and for the most part, he's good to me. He's funny, smart, and my dad loves him."

"Sounds like a great guy," I reply. My Adam's apple ties itself in a knot.

"He really is..." She hesitates.

"I hate to bring it up, but does he know you're here? About our little pact that if we married other people, we'd cheat on them with each other?" I chuckle at the sheer immaturity of our former selves.

"Oh, God. We *did* say that, didn't we? We were such kids back then."

"I know. It's been so long, but it's yesterday in my mind."

Every person surrounding us is laughing, chewing, and carrying their newfound treasures. I could be viewing a snapshot of our former lives; nothing has changed— except these two men. They don't fit inside the photograph—an abnormality, a smudge. They walk briskly together, wearing almost identical outfits, dark sunglasses masking the majority of their expressionless faces.

They both have backpacks—

"I can't believe I'm saying this about myself—Casey and I divorced months ago and haven't spoken since." Her chin digs into her chest. "Shortly after the wedding, I knew things weren't right. But by that point, it was too late. I mean, we got *married.* Things were great while we dated, but every night following our vows, when I crawled into bed with him, I'd try to convince myself that this wasn't *settling.* It's just what people do. But it *was* settling. It is." That same single tear rolls down her cheek, and the clock rewinds to our last encounter. "I didn't mean to lie to you, but it's a hard thing to admit. I don't ever want you to think less of me. But what should I have done? Say *no* to a man who loves me to keep waiting around, hoping—"

"No." Our eyes meet. "Like you said, this was all meant to happen. *Everything*, no matter how horrible and pointless that may sound. Maybe our suffering was necessary to show us the way, to make us grow, to show us what we truly desire."

"And what do *you* desire now that you've had all this time to grow? All this time to reflect?" She wipes the backside of her hand against her cheek. Her ring draws a thin red line.

*This is my chance and I'm not letting it pass by.* "You, that's all. Everything I'll ever want and need is standing right in front of me. You're the only thing I've *ever* desired. My life lost its purpose the day you walked out the door. I've been searching for you ever since, but never expected to find you. Yet, here we are. I didn't realize it or appreciate you before, and I regret it with every breath I take. I just want you to keep smiling, even if it's not because of me."

Luna replies, "I could never seem to forget you. Maybe it's because we never had any real closure, or it could be something else. But every time I'd get close to forgetting, you would *flash* somewhere. It sounds silly, but your name, someone that resembled you, or something completely random would pop up when I least expected it. I never looked for it, but it always found me."

"You probably won't believe me, but I know *exactly*

what you mean." I glance into her hairline, the globe-trekking dispensary of bobby pins. "You've *never* left my mind. I've wished for this exact moment every day since you left, for one more second with you."

Our hands find one another; her touch is electric. Her dainty fingers rub against mine as she says, "This feels like we never stopped, as if we could pick up right where we left off."

I am weightless; her grip is the sole thing keeping me on the ground.

"What are we doing?" I ask.

"Anything we want," she replies. "You were always the love of my life."

She's the blood in my veins, the air in my lungs. "Forever, Tick."

We walk together, side by side, hand in hand. My smile is so wide it hurts. My blushed cheeks are pinned to my eyelids. My facial muscles have become weak from underuse, the happiness conjuring pinched agony. The pain I happily welcome for the rest of my life.

The ache of love, the sting of living.

Pedestrians walk nonchalantly past this monumental occasion in our lives, oblivious that they are an unpaid extra in my life's greatest scene. Witnesses to our history, all so professional, never directing their shifting glances toward the camera.

I guess there *are* perfect moments in life, after all. Or maybe everybody only receives one.

I know this is mine.

How many moments like this have *I* witnessed and failed to acknowledge? How many times have I been a bystander as others are immersed in their own life-changing memory? They happen all around me: sadness, happiness, love. I want to recognize them all. I want everyone to experience their own version of this occurrence, to be alive with the one they adore, in the place they love, under the most perfect, effervescent sundown.

I glance at Luna just to see her smile as the purple sunset projects a kaleidoscope of vibrant pigments within her retinas. *I am peaceful.*

Screaming. Shouting in a muffled language I can't seem to understand.

A high-pitched shriek echoes off the cobblestones.

Our grip tightens.

# PART III

# WITHOUT AN END

## 1

**H**ow long have *I been trapped in solitude?*
*How much longer could I possibly exist*
*before dying of starvation, both of the body*
*and the mind?*

Although I didn't witness its birth or death, I know the darkness of this place bloomed like a diseased black sunflower in hell, its jagged, unnatural petals extending, and spreading tiny witch fingers into the obscured night sky. A world that rests but never sleeps.

My sanity is merely a suggestion, my life's memories are the sole sense of rationality in this place. My remaining senses pick up the slack from my sight as an abrupt sound emerges—the first noise I've heard in what could be years. *I'm saved!* "HELP ME, PLEASE!" I shriek to no avail. Additional arbitrary noises follow, and I can almost pinpoint their direction.

CLUNK!

Powerful light, dwarfing the power of ten thousand solar eclipses, crashes into this world.

*I wasn't blind after all, but now I might be.*

The light has such intensity I can hear it. It's *all* I can hear. Shining. Radiating. A bleached world. The violent light washes over my body, awakening every dulled sense. Its deafening buzzing muffles the sound of a faraway conversation. "After—steps are complete—final prepar—any questions?" a voice says.

A second voice responds, "No, but I'm looking forw—sewing the—sh—one day."

I can hear more with each passing moment.

The first voice responds, "You'll get your opportunity, more than you'll care to count. Like I told you, I'm an old-fashioned kinda guy; the pin gun has never failed me. But you're free to use any method your heart desires: suture, pillow under the neck, or just a necktie around their head. Kind of looks like one of those old-timey toothache bandages if you ask me, but whatever does the job."

*Sewing?*

Cloudy shapes float through the blinding white sky where I've been hovering endlessly in darkness. My vision continues to adjust to the bright surroundings, and I can now discern that two men are standing behind me, one older and one younger. "Well, as always with this profession, we're on a time crunch. Let's go ahead and begin," the older man commands.

*Begin what?*

Movement, as if on a conveyor belt, slides me backwards. My dilated eyes calibrate themselves as I'm extracted from some type of storage compartment, the darkness giving birth to me. The sliding stops with a jarring, mechanical THUD. Large, orb light fixtures stare back as the realization occurs that, for some reason, I'm facing the ceiling.

*Where the hell am I? And what are these people doing to me?*

"Hand me that sheet, please." Fabric rustles and snaps. "Thanks a bunch. Always try to keep the private parts covered as much as you can. We don't want any funny business going on or even a slight suspicion of—you know—*things* happening down here. You understand."

"I'm not sure I follow-"

A clogged throat coughs to clear the path. "For instance, relations that shouldn't happen between someone like us and someone like *this*. Without going into the not-so-juicy details, we had a problem a couple years back with one of our staff, and we never want to go down that road again. Let's just say he was a bit too fond of his job and leave it at that. Comprende?"

"You got it, boss," the younger man replies.

"Now, you can leave the *rest* of them uncovered—don't have to worry about them getting chilly," the old man continues. "But remember, the easiest way to remain successful in this line of work is to always—and I mean *always*—remember that these were people. Somebody out there loved this now lifeless vessel, and it's our job to give them closure. You'll come across all shapes and sizes of all sorts of *parts*, but always remember: treat these people the way you'd like to be treated, because I can assure you one thing, my friend—one day you'll be on this roller with *your* tiny pecker showing."

The younger man replies, "Gotcha, boss. You don't ever have to worry about me getting frisky. I've got a girl at home that keeps me plenty busy in the bedroom. I'm always down to try new things, but plugging a stiff has never been on the bucket list."

The old man nods. "Glad to hear it. Let's pick up where we left off." In unison, the two men count down from three. When the number *one* strikes, the men strain as they lift my body toward the lights; engorged veins zigzag across their flesh. My body rises, levitating inside of their obscured grip until they place me on another flat surface. *Why didn't I feel that?*

*Why don't I feel anything?*

There must be something here, something about these two men, *anything* about this situation that could help make sense of it. They're both wearing scrubs, the textile a soft heather gray, yet they appear much different than I remember, almost resembling windbreakers.

"As you witnessed with this particular case, the wounds did the majority of fluid drainage work for us, but you won't always be that lucky. There's no such thing as an *easy* case; some will need this and some will need that. Some folks go out fairly clean—as clean as one could hope. But the others, boy, they make a mess out of themselves for us to mop up."

He pauses, his cheeks flashing pale with raw memory.

"Anyways, each case is unique, and you'll learn something new with every embalming. Hell, even after thirty-three years in this business, just when I think I've seen it all, BOOM, something unprecedented comes rolling through those double doors. So, strap on your learnin' cap because I'm gonna teach you how to suture the most impossible laceration, administer an endless foray of injections, and drumroll please—show you how to do makeup better than all of your girlfriends combined!"

This earns a healthy laugh from the younger man.

"Ya see, a good sense of humor in this business will keep you sane. But don't expect the people down here to laugh at any of your jokes. I've been working on them for over three decades and nothing! Tough crowd!"

*There's nothing worse than being a third wheel.* The entire time they've been having this conversation, we have been moving. I don't know this because I've felt it, I *know* this because lights are passing overhead and I doubt it's the building moving and not us. *Wait, did he just say embalm? And what wound? I'm in no pain. I'm alive, you idiots!* How could they not know I'm alive? My eyes have been darting from side to side this entire time. *Look down at me! Here, I'll start blinking like a maniac!* My eyes flutter with speed that would force a hummingbird to quit his day job. Still nothing. As my desperation becomes more pronounced, the lights stop moving. They've positioned the table underneath a straight line of three hanging lamps, an all-white stoplight.

*Okay, blinking didn't work. I have to move.* With every possible ounce of energy, I attempt to will my legs, arms, mouth or *anything* to make the smallest amount of motion. It seems so simple for my mind to command the muscles into action. The electrical signals are sent through my body, soaring and bouncing through every cell, but there is no response. There is a broken connection; I'm paralyzed. My entire body feels asleep, yet my mind is fully awake. In fact, it feels *more* awake than ever before.

*Is this anesthesia gone wrong?* I've read about this: patients going in for invasive surgery, feeling every injection, every incision, every bone breaking. The ignorant doctors open their chests, using razor sharp shears to cut through countless layers of muscle, flesh, and fat, their rib cage swinging open like saloon doors, gloved digits crudely rooting, extracting, and rearranging vital organs and sensitive tissue. Every piece kept under strict lock and key, never meant to be touched. The poor soul is left without a choice, forced to remain inside and suffer. Hoping to pass out. Praying to die.

"What size shoe did you say he was?" the younger man shouts.

"Umm, looks like a *petite* 9 ½ to me. You'll get pretty good at eyeballing people's boot sizes—another priceless talent." The old man chuckles at his own cleverness.

9 ½ *wide,* asshole. *What the hell do I need shoes for?*

The younger man trots off to fetch the mysterious shoes, and while he is gone, the older man glides his rolling stool toward my lower body and out of sight. I hear a package crinkle and then sense swaying. My vision rocks back and forth as his breathing spells signs of difficulty. I don't even want to imagine what he's doing now, but I may need to file a sexual assault report after this.

"Tighty-whities, huh? Definitely not built for comfort," the young man exclaims upon re-entering the room.

The old man responds, "Yes, not my preference either. It's more of a formality than anything."

*They're dressing me. Why on earth are they doing this? There has been a terrible, horrible mistake. I can dress myself, and yes, I hate tighty-whities!*

"Want to throw those socks on our friend here?" the older man asks of his new subordinate.

"Sure thing, boss. I've got two little brothers back home, so this is nothing new for me—well, I guess it's a *little* different!" The older man belts out a crackling, phlegmy laugh.

After the socks, come the pants—that is the natural order of things, but this is about as far from natural as anything could be. The two men combine their efforts to shimmy a pair of pants up to my waist.

"Careful with that crease. Don't let 'er bunch up too

much, or these trousers will look like they were snatched out of a hamper in no time," the old man instructs. "Now onto the torso. You can get by with one person on the lower half, but it goes a *lot* smoother with two people working on the top. Believe me, it can turn into a real comedy skit. Here's how we'll go about this: you'll get a good grip and lift 'em up to a seated position. Now, this ain't as easy as it sounds; that boy is gonna want to go this way and that. It's your job to keep him as steady as possible while I get this shirt on."

*This is my chance. They'll be forced to look at my eyes. Then they'll see. God, I hope they see.*

"You can handle that, right?"

"Yeah, no problem," the younger man responds as he shoves an arm underneath my back, causing my vision to nod in agreement. His opposite arm grabs ahold of my right shoulder, and in an instant, I'm seated upright. *Now is my best shot.* I begin to scramble my eyes in every possible way, blinking like I've never blinked before, bulging my retinas like a cartoon character after placing a four-fingered hand on a red-hot stove.

Despite my efforts, the young man focuses his undivided attention on observing the older man's clothing technique. *Have you never put a shirt on before? Holy shit, how tough could it be?* As fast as they sat me up, they're laying me back down. The two men fumble with the buttons on what appears to be a white collared dress shirt.

"Looking sharp. Now let's get it tucked in nice and tight, but be gentle with that sensitive spot—good. Next is the jacket, and we'll do it the same way." The process repeats, and I fail once more in making them notice me. Their concealed hands dance atop my torso, concluding their adjustments to my fancy new attire.

After a pause, both in motion and sound, the older man requests a mirror. A large, extendable mirror unfolds from a nearby wall. The young man pulls the object backward, stretching its mechanical arms, the silver device chasing his retreating footsteps. He positions the mirror directly in front of my face. *See, you dumb bastards, my eyes—*

*My eyes are closed.*

They're not only closed, they appear *held* shut. Permanently. *How can I see my reflection with my eyes closed?* Looking over the rest of my face, it appears stoic, expressionless, lifeless. I'm trapped within a wax figure of myself.

"Let's brush up on those makeup skills, shall we? Watch the master at work, young buck," the older man boasts. As he begins to apply foundation to brighten up my lackluster appearance, I can't help but gaze at the ghastly reflection within the mirror's beveled borders. *If my eyes aren't open and I'm dead, how can I see?* A strange suspicion occurs that I'm not *seeing* through my eyes at all, but rather *absorbing* the surroundings through my forehead.

*How does that make any sense? Is this what happens when you die?* I've never heard of an afterlife where one gets trapped behind a makeup-caked brow for all eternity. Or maybe I only exist until my body no longer does. When I start decomposing, my awareness will slowly wither away with it. My flesh and consciousness will be eaten away by the maggots, bacteria, and every other flesh eater who desires to feast on my embalmed, chemical-ridden corpse. At least there is no physical pain. Maybe they'll cremate me, all my worries turning to ash in an instant, a fast-forward to my second death. It'll be strange to die again, because I don't remember the first time. But maybe that's a good thing.

"Vwol-Ahh!" the old man poorly pronounces. "Was I right, or was I right?"

The apprentice mumbles concurrence.

"The old lady is always nagging me, saying I should leave this dingy, decrepit place and head off to the big city to do famous people's makeup. I keep telling her, there's one problem with that–I don't have any customer reviews!"

The apprentice chuckles.

The old man leans close to my face and shouts, "Whaddya' say, mister? Mind if I get your headshot for my portfolio?" This triggers that cracking, smoker's laugh, the phlegm popping like chewing gum within his gyrating throat.

What an unbelievingly annoying afterlife. I'm pissed off at the drunk driver that veered into my lane to kill me, or the pimple-faced high-schooler who assembled the chunky ham sandwich I choked on, or the gray meteor that fell from the corner of the universe just to crush me, or *whatever* is responsible for making me spend any amount of time with these two idiots.

"Okay, we're about done here. We have an hour until guests arrive, so let's position him in the hall and make sure everything is good to go. Get this buttoned up, and let's hot step it, I'm starving," the old man says. The apprentice lets out a labored sigh and a wooden slab begins elevating from beside my lower left leg. The wood cascades over my thighs like an Alaskan sunset and closes overtop, meeting the table.

*No, this isn't a table.* Regular tables don't have fluffy, white cushioned and tufted liners.

This is a *casket.*

*No, no, no.* An earth-shattering hurricane brews within my nonexistent gut. *I've been in a casket this whole fucking time?*

It's real now. All hope is gone. This isn't the 1800's; they don't put live people in burial boxes—not to mention embalming them first. I'm dead. It's really over. I'll never speak to anyone again. I'll never see my family. I'll never love again.

Imprisoned within the body I've betrayed, now doomed to my eternal, ironic punishment.

Life is short, the *after*life is not.

<u>2</u>

Lights begin moving overhead again as the young man wheels me through the chocolate-brown threshold of a tunneled doorway. I'm unsure of what to do with myself, how I should feel about being dead, and what other surprises are in store.

I'm entirely at the will of these two strangers as they prepare their own morbid version of show-and-tell. *Look what we did. We made a really dead person look presentable. Not so much* alive—*that would be creepy—but alive enough where he doesn't frighten the children. The finest line to walk of all. Now, we're going to wheel him out for everyone's aesthetic enjoyment like a dessert tray in a five-star restaurant.* The customers' eyes bigger than their stomachs.

Corpse brûlée. Apple don't-turnover. Formalde pie. *Hope everyone saved room.*

The notion of attending my own funeral has at least given me something to look forward to. *Who will be in attendance? Whose true colors will be revealed?*

Weaving through the hallways of the funeral home, I watch as it transforms from a medical workplace into a place for mourning. The walls start off bare, but the farther we journey, pictures begin appearing along the drywall—depictions of fellow dead men like me, only these holy men have halos around their heads.

The apprentice slows the ride to shimmy through a thick wooden doorway. A rear wheel catches and crudely bounces off the trim, jarring the carrier. The worry in his voice is apparent as he says, "Okay— nobody saw that."

*I did, but don't worry, my lips are sealed.*

He wheels the casket into a large room with a vaulted ceiling and a large stained-glass chandelier hanging overhead. My straining peripherals notice that both sides of the room are lined with floral arrangements and colorful balloons. *Wow, somebody must've been loved in here before me.* Although I have no sense of smell, I bet this room reeks of flowers—the kind of overpowering aroma that ruins flowers for a person for life because of the strong association with death. Stopping to smell a beautiful wildflower years from now, the brain will trigger an ancient, instinctive survival trait that transports them back to the exact time of their loved one's demise. Each time they sniff a rose, their freshly healed wound is ripped open once again. They'll train themselves to avoid these scents, sacrificing the sweet smell of nature for the peaceful sake of closure.

The young man positions my burial box perpendicular within the room and abruptly exits stage left. *What, no small talk? Rude. Was he expecting a tip?*

I find myself alone again and bored.

The funeral setting conjures a bizarre memory from my childhood.

When I was seven years old, my uncle passed away from a fatal heart attack. It caught the entire family off guard, despite the man smoking to start each morning and drinking to end each night. But I suppose those were the days before anyone knew any better—a hindsight is 20/20 sort of thing. Although I'd experienced death in animals, this was the first encounter that warranted a funeral.

I remember being confused and distraught about the entire process. I didn't know my uncle well, but I was still upset. Because if he could die, that meant my mother could die, my father could die, *I* could die. That's when mortality began to set in, and it scared the bejesus outta me. The finality, the weight of it, the feeling of wanting to stay but having no choice but to leave, like getting kicked out of your own party. It was making me sick, and the more I thought about it, the more unanswered questions I had.

My family misinterpreted my anxiety for grief. Looking back, I understand their position. Here I was, a kid asking all of these awful questions when their loved one just died. My mother assured me that when the funeral was over, all of my concerns would be answered. I believed her. I walked down the aisle in a black suit, despite originally choosing my favorite baseball jersey, and I saw him lying there. I'd never seen a dead person before, just fake ones in movies. Only his face was visible, a bumpy silhouette of recognizable features seated atop the crest of the coffin. The sight stopped me in my tracks—my muscles locked, a thousand scarabs burrowing beneath my cheeks. My mother pinched my arm, whispering a reminder of our car-ride discussion. My flat-soled shoes became ice skates as I glided down the aisle with her pulling on my wrist. But the closer we neared the coffin, the more beautiful it appeared. Oddly beautiful. I couldn't help but think about the person who'd crafted such a thing, spent endless hours carving the intricate details, only for it to be buried in a dirty hole with a decaying person inside. I knew better than to bring up such matters at the moment. Then I stared at him, my uncle, lying inside of that box. I recalled him falling asleep on our recliner after Thanksgiving dinner the previous year, his fingers interlaced against his stomach, his creased eyes relaxed, his mouth made of stone. He looked exactly as he did that night.

I couldn't believe it. I expected a monster from a horror movie, but it was only my uncle. Well, maybe a little faded. I half-expected him to flex his eyelids and turn his head to thank me for coming. *A penny for your thoughts.* But he didn't. He was silent and inert as I whispered a farewell to his body.

My mother's voice spoiled the mild moment. "Now, I want you to kiss your uncle goodbye." *What?* I told her I didn't want to, that I was fine with being here now, but I didn't want to kiss him. "It's the best way for closure, and we're not walking away until you say goodbye. *Don't* make a scene." Her grip tightened on my arm; I could feel a bruise forming on the bone. I looked at him. He appeared so old at that moment. I couldn't bear the thought of putting my lips on him, but I knew better than to disagree with my mother, especially in her grief. I lifted myself against the edge of the coffin and leaned over to be face-to-face with him, looking directly into his sunken eyes. Fright quivered my flesh. I was terrified of falling in, that he would grab me, or those eyes would snap open. Childish fears, but petrifying all the same. "It'll make you feel better." My lips puckered, just as I'd practiced on my hand when I dreamed of my elementary school crush, rehearsing for my first kiss with an older girl, imagining how magical it would feel to have her lips against mine, never picturing that my first kiss would be with my deceased uncle. My pursed lips landed on the corner of my uncle's glued mouth; his coldness sent a shiver down my spine, like it was transferred into me. So permanent, so final. I knew he'd never be warm again. I pulled my dry mouth away and lowered to the floor, absent of my body. My mother led me away. "I'm proud of you. I knew you'd feel better." But I didn't. I was led away and more than a little traumatized.

I sat silent during the funeral, recounting the events. My mother assumed I was mourning my relative. What I was *really* mourning was my innocence, because once it was gone, it could never be regained. It was horrible, but one good thing came from it: I discovered what love was. I cared deeply for my uncle as any child does, but with that kiss, I learned I didn't love him. I know it seems cruel, but I think people only want to kiss a deceased person if they truly love them. That is a small, exclusive group—the absolute most important people in the world. That's the definition of love you won't find in the dictionary. I knew that was a beautiful thing, but it was a loss I prayed I'd never be forced to experience. With my uncle's passing, I had experienced death, but not true loss. From that moment on, it was only a matter of time until I'd be embraced by the cold arms of a faceless stranger, and Death would be her name.

*Wait—*

Footsteps enter the room accompanied by a whispered conversation. "We must be early. Where would you like to sit?" the anonymous voices ask.

*Don't be shy.*

One after another, featureless visitors enter the room, and I'm left here wondering who might be in attendance to view the exhibit. One completed minute bleeds into the next, all crawling at a snail's pace. Nobody has approached me, and I don't blame them; dead people creep me out, too, and I'm deader than disco. The hissed conversations grow so entwined that it's impossible to follow a single voice. The mashed sounds are turning this into a dull affair for *me*, the star of this attraction. *I've always been fascinated with mummies, but I never fathomed becoming one.*

God, I wish I could shush these—*there's a hand inside my cushiony box.* It's a dainty hand, wrapped in thin, leather-bound skin, crisscrossed with plump, blue veins. A single splash of clear liquid bursts out of the weathered, boney knuckles. "It'll make you feel better."

Raising my gaze upwards past a plain black dress, my mother is staring back at me. Her face is unrecognizable, covered in flowing tears and smeared mascara, appearing as though she's aged ten years since I last saw her. *When was that?* As she sobs an incoherent mumble, I try to comfort the woman who gave me life.

*I'm in no pain, Mom. Please stop crying!*

Her trembling hands grip the edge of the casket as she leans closer to my barren body. Her vibrating lips press against my numbed face, remaining there, breathing heavily through her flaring nostrils. She pulls away, a stream of liquid attached between us. Her quivering mouth struggles to hold the delicate structure of language together. "You can't be gone. I don't *believe* it. W-w—why would this happen to you? Not my son. I'm so sorry—I'm so sorry, Ardy."

This is torture.

Every other obstacle I've endured was paradise in comparison. *This* is hell. All I want is to reassure my heartbroken mother that I'm okay, even though it would be a lie. Similar to the darkness of the morgue, I never fathomed there could be such desolation, how I could be this powerless. I lie here helpless as her grief-filled tears soak into the fine, woven fabric of the last outfit I'll ever wear. "My baby, not my baby boy."

*Does everyone experience this?* What kind of a horrible, cynical afterlife could this be? The premise of nothingness after death now seems like pure bliss. A pair of large hands wrap around her delicate shoulders, pulling her away from me and into their mortal embrace. *Dad.* He glances at me for a moment before he leads my devastated mother away. "It will be all right, honey. No one can hurt him now," he says.

"They did, though. How could something so horrible happen to our *baby?*" she replies with salty anger in her tone. She's ushered away before I can hear the rest of the exchange.

*So horrible? What happened to me?* My final *alive* memories are nowhere to be found.

Why can't I remember anything? My brain is so overloaded with sensory outputs that a thick veil of fog has overtaken my memory, as if it is no longer necessary, irrelevant. One would assume that without the burden of operating my flesh and bone body, my brain would be running at full speed, but it's not. Maybe it takes practice to get better at being dead. I *am* new at this and have never been a fast learner.

*Think hard.* All I see is Luna.

This is nothing new because her image appears every time my eyes close. Only, she and I are walking—

While fighting this internal losing battle, I realize the funeral has begun. *Here, just listen to these people to find out what the hell did this to me—not that I'll be*

187

*able to do anything about it.*

A man's voice says, "What is a lifetime? We use the term as a form of measurement that supposedly applies to everyone. A universal fit. But is it accurate? Is it fair? Let's face it, my lifetime won't be the same as your lifetime, and yours unequal to hers. Each of us is unique, each made special from the moment of conception—the way we speak, laugh, love, and even the time we are given. *Lifetimes* are never long enough, especially in unfortunate circumstances such as these. Some lifetimes last longer and others are shorter, but the important thing to remember is that there *is* life. There *is* love. And although our bodies may fade, the impact we leave on other's lives will last forever."

A throat clears in an otherwise hushed room.

"Now, we will invite Arden's mother to give the eulogy. Please bear with her and give her strength. She needs all you can offer right now."

I can't do this. As hard as giving my eulogy will be for my mother, it will be equally as difficult for me to hear it, knowing I'm the one causing her so much pain. If I was alive right now, I would kill myself to escape, but only to find myself trapped once again!

Paper crinkles and rustles on the stage. The motherly, soothing voice from my childhood begins. "Wh—w–what can I ever say about Ardy that you don't already know? He was his own man, always against the grain. He left a lasting imprint on every life he touched, filled everyone with love at every opportunity, and now his loss has left a hole in all of us. He had the world at his fingertips and nothing was out of his reach—" *More paper crinkling.* "I can't *read* this any longer. My written words no longer feel appropriate, so I'll go with what feels right."

A heavy breath is inhaled through clogged nostrils. "No parent should be forced to bury their child like this, *ever.* It goes without saying that my heart, my world, is crushed. My life stopped when I received that phone call, as I'm sure yours did as well. Watching the event unfold on the news—I'm sorry—it felt like I was watching a movie. A horrible, horrible movie about some twisted fictional reality that needed to be turned off. A movie that some sick, demented mind had written to profit off of some earth-shattering tragedy. But I couldn't turn it off; just like you couldn't either. This is our reality. Before, when I'd see something like this happen in the world, it would be to *other* people. It was always those nameless, distant *other* people this affected, not us. *That kind of stuff can't happen to my family.* You pray for the victims, talk about it at work for a day or so, and then go on with your normal life as if nothing ever happened. Meanwhile, those families were suffering, just as we are now. Out there is somebody who is seeing *this* event unfold and thinking of *us* as the *other* people. I pray they never learn any different. I know it's wrong to envy, but I envy them. I would give anything to be naive again. I would give *anything* to have my son again. I'm so sorry, honey. *Please* don't take my sunshine away."

189

I cannot feel physical sensations, yet this is agony. Everything is paralyzed besides my emotions—the one thing that can never be taken away. This whole time, I've been here, lying inside my casket, listening to my mother pour out her soul. *I must go to her and tell her that I love her! I must get out of this box.*

With concentrated effort, I begin pushing against my forehead. Strong, electric vibrations echo throughout my being. The shock generates such fear that I stop pressing, and the sensation ceases. *What the hell was that? Whatever it was, it was* something. That is the first physical sensation I've had since this whole ordeal began.

My mother continues to sob as the voices begin to lead her away from the stage. I must try again. This time I won't stop pushing no matter what.

I begin pushing once more, and even after anticipating the shock, the uncomfortable sensation rivals the first attempt, vibrating with such ferocity that the notion of my former teeth shattering like glass seems inevitable. Struggling with the aching, horrendous sensation, I strain to find the will to continue. The pain is too much to bear. My soul is being viciously torn apart at the seams.

But then, the stunning realization occurs that I can now see *over* the casket's edge. *Oh my God, I'm moving!* With my new progression, I give one last desperate push, expending every scrap of energy I have left. The intensity trumps the original power, but there's no going back. For once, I'm committed to moving forward, no matter the cost. Face the pain, face the demons, face the fear, and face life—even if it *is* over.

The vibrations morph into an extreme tearing sensation that deafens my world with the scream of a thousand unraveling rolls of duct tape. The vibrations subside to a slow aftershock, mimicking the sensation of an asleep limb that is waking up.

My clenched eyes open to find I'm now standing, facing the crowd. With clear vision, I watch three men escort my collapsing mother into her seat.

A heavyset, sweaty man approaches the stage; he is bee-lining, charging toward me. For an instant, I'm positive he'll run right into me, until he pivots for the podium at the last possible second. I'm standing right behind him, among burning candles, baskets of flowers, and my former body.

I can smell the flowers; the nectar is extravagant. Each arrangement is equipped with a different scent. I can pinpoint them all. The powerful sensations are intoxicating, almost as if I've never smelled before.

The perspiring man—likely the funeral director—attempts to hold the procession together. He reassures the somber crowd I'm in a better place and we should all be comforted that my suffering is over.

*If he only knew.*

Looking out amongst the crowd, I notice so many familiar faces–long, lost figures that molded me into the person I was. None of these countless arrangements of facial features are looking at me. Except one.

Luna stands in the center aisle, wearing the same sunflower dress she wore the night of her housewarming party.

*She can't see me, right?* I wave with a slight flick of my wrist, and she responds with a smile and a playful shake of her head. *How can she—* Luna nods to my right side. Following her direction, I see myself, lying in the casket, looking peaceful, young, and healthy. *Considering.* I must admit, the two knuckleheads did a good job on me.

*But why is there another casket beside mine?* Moving toward the rectangular burial box, I see the all-too-familiar face. The face I see when I'm awake, the face I meet in my favorite dreams, the only one that ever mattered. *Dead.*

*No. I've accepted being gone, but not her. Please not her.*

A presence approaches. Luna is staring down at her former self. The serene reflection off a still pond. Directing her attention deep within my eyes, I hear, "*They* are *better than me at doing makeup. Took you long enough to get out. I've been waiting. I bet you struggled with the pain, didn't you? You always were a little pansy.*" She says without the slightest motion of her lips.

Judging my dumbfounded expression, she continues. *"Go ahead and try it. Tell me something, anything you want. No one will hear, just us. We're connected now. We're connected to* everything. *Speak not with your mouth, but with your true self."* This makes absolutely no sense, yet it makes perfect sense. *"I love you, too, and yes, I've never felt better,"* she replies to a thought I didn't even know I had.

Staring into her perfectly round, forest green eyes, all my troubles melt away. An overwhelming sense of complete peacefulness covers me like a childhood blanket. The entire universe is in her eyes, and I sense we now have the ability to travel to its most distant places. *"You do,"* Luna replies without either of us saying a word. *"We can go anywhere: the moon, Saturn, another galaxy,"* she continues with a half-smile, *"but first, I think somebody wanted to show me the Pyramids."* She knows my reply without a sound.

She takes my hand, leading me down the center aisle as the funeral director speaks. "This beloved couple, held together in life by love, shall now be bound together for eternity."

My mother is hunched over in her aisle seat, sobbing into her palms, gasping in erratic bursts of panicked breath. Standing beside her, I place my left hand on the shoulder of the woman who carried me in her body for nine months, the woman who sacrificed everything she had for my well-being, the heroic woman who gave every bit of love in her heart to her child. *Thank you, Mom. There's never been a better mother in the world, and don't worry, I am in a better place. Nothing could have prevented this. We'll see each other again. I love you.* As I release my hand from her shoulder, her breathing slows. She raises her head from her hands, her eyes twinkle with moisture, and her back presses against the chair as she takes a deep breath, exhaling with a faint smile.

I turn to see Luna's arms spread around two people, squeezing tight with her invisible hands. She pulls away, revealing the strained faces of her heartbroken father and her former husband. She turns to me, her cheeks dimple, a single, flowing tear landing between her pursed lips.

The swimming silence echoes through my soul. I know it's time to *go.*

Walking hand in hand through the solemn crowd of loved ones from our former lives, I've never been happier. All those unknown feelings and indescribable sensations are no longer so; they are all here, every joyous, stomach-fluttering emotion from my dream encounters with Luna, existing forever, all wrapped up into one.

*Serenity.*

"—permit those who are responsible for this savage attack, and all those like it around the world, to be punished by the hands of justice and by the will of God—" I hear the man speak these words, yet the sounds no longer possess meaning. All that matters is now.

Approaching the glass exit doors at the end of the aisle, a peculiar reflection is staring back at us. We don't see each other walking and holding hands as one would anticipate.

Blue lights.

We are a pair of floating orbs, bursting with thousands of endless rays of magnificent sapphire beams. Every possible hue, tint, and tone of the color, all at once. Infinite.

Beautiful, spectacular colors that have never existed in my world before, but now I'm certain I wouldn't survive without them. "*This is the real me, and that's the real you,*" I hear internally while studying the glowing reflection. I notice our beams are interwoven. "*I told you we were connected. We've* always *been. Now, quit gawking at the goods and let's go.*"

Without another moment's hesitation or thought, our vibrant blue, blurry reflections rapidly approach, the two versions colliding for an instant, as we glide effortlessly through the door.

Made in the USA
Middletown, DE
19 May 2019